Be appalled, Alina, Demyan thought.

Gather your things now and we'll head back to the car, he half hoped, for she was innocent and he was far from that.

Instead Alina took another drink of water.

He watched her tongue lick over her lips, and it was not a seductive move, but he felt it in his groin.

"Is that why nothing shocks you?" Alina asked, and he watched as her cheeks turned to fire.

"What do you mean?"

"Well..." Alina didn't know how to voice it, so she spoke about herself. "Everything shocks me. Maybe I was too sheltered. I mean..."

"We're taking about sex, yes?" Demyan needlessly checked. He loved that even her throat was red, and then he thought of her breasts.

And whether or not it was convenient, Demyan was turned on at the thought of her shyness giving way to defiance.

All about the author...
Carol Marinelli

CAROL MARINELLI finds writing a bio rather like writing her New Year's resolutions. Oh, she would love to say that since she wrote the last one she now goes to the gym regularly and doesn't stop for coffee and cake and a gossip afterward; that she's incredibly organized and writes for a few productive hours a day after tidying her immaculate house and a brisk walk with the dog.

The reality is, Carol spends an inordinate amount of time daydreaming about dark, brooding men and exotic places (research), which doesn't leave too much time for the gym, housework or anything that comes in between, and her most productive writing hours happen to be in the middle of the night, which leaves her in a constant state of bewildered exhaustion.

Originally from England, Carol now lives in Melbourne, Australia. She adores going back to the U.K. for a visit— actually, she adores going anywhere for a visit—and constantly (expensively) strives to overcome her fear of flying. She has three gorgeous children, who are growing up so fast (too fast—they've just worked out that she lies about her age!) and keep her busy with a never-ending round of homework, sport and friends coming over.

A nurse and a writer, Carol writes for the Harlequin Presents® and Harlequin Medical Romance lines and is passionate about both. She loves the fast-paced, busy setting of a modern hospital, but every now and then admits it's bliss to escape to the glamorous, alluring world of her Presents heroes and heroines. A bit like her real life actually!

Other titles by Carol Marinelli available in ebook:

THE PLAYBOY OF PUERTO BANÚS
A LEGACY OF SECRETS *(Sicily's Corretti Dynasty)*
PLAYING THE DUTIFUL WIFE
BEHOLDEN TO THE THRONE *(Empire of the Sands)*

Carol Marinelli

—

The Only Woman to Defy Him

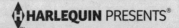

Recycling programs
for this product may
not exist in your area.

ISBN-13: 978-0-373-13240-9

THE ONLY WOMAN TO DEFY HIM

First North American Publication 2014

Printed in U.S.A.

The Only Woman to Defy Him

PROLOGUE

JUST NOT TODAY.

Demyan Zukov looked out the window of his private jet as his plane began its final descent into Sydney, Australia.

It truly was a magnificent view and Demyan owned part of the skyline. His dark eyes located his penthouse then he moved his pensive gaze to the numerous inlets that beckoned as temptingly as a sensual finger. The water was a stunning deep blue and was filled with boats, ferries and yachts that streaked their way through the harbour, leaving long white tails behind them. Always the view both exhilarated and excited Demyan. Always there was the prospect of good times ahead as his plane came in to land.

Just not today.

As he gazed down, for once unmoved by the spectacular sight, Demyan recalled the very first time that he had come to Australia. It had been in far less grand style and certainly there had been no press waiting to greet him. He had entered the country unknown, yet quietly determined to make his mark. Demyan had been just thirteen years old when he had left Russia for the first and last time.

He had sat at the back of a commercial jet in economy, beside his aunt, Katia. As he had looked out the window, as he had glimpsed for the first time the land that awaited him, and Katia had spoken about the farm in the Blue Mountains that would soon be his home, Demyan had scarcely known how to hope.

Demyan's upbringing had been brutal and harsh. He had not known who his father was and Demyan's single mother had found herself trapped in a downward spiral of poverty and alcohol. The small support she had received from the government had gone towards feeding Annika's habit.

When Demyan had been five and his mother had lost her spot at the market, it had been Demyan who had taken on the responsibility of providing for them. Demyan had worked hard, and not just at school. At evenings and weekends he'd teamed up with a street boy, Mikael, and cleaned car windows at traffic lights uninvited, as well as begging tourists for spare change.

When necessary he would rummage through the garbage at the back of restaurants and hotels. Somehow, most nights, there had been a meal of sorts for himself and Annika. Not that his mother had bothered with eating near the end of her life—instead it had been vodka and more vodka as she'd grown increasingly paranoid and superstitious and demanded that her son conform to the rituals that she'd felt kept her world safe.

On her death, Demyan had fully expected to join Mikael on the streets but instead his mother's sister Katia had come from Australia, where she'd lived, to Russia for her sister's burial.

'Annika always told me that you were both doing well.' Katia was appalled when she found out how her sister and nephew had been living. 'In her letters and phone calls…' Katia's voice trailed off as she looked at the sparse living conditions when she entered their flat, and then she looked properly at her desperately thin nephew. His black hair and grey eyes were such a contrast to his waxy pale skin and though Demyan refused to cry, confusion, suspicion and grief were etched on his face—never more so than at Annika's burial.

Despite Demyan's best efforts to ease his mother's mind by obliging and going along with her many superstitions and rituals it had not been considered a *good* death. At the burial the two mourners stood silent beside Annika's grave. The bleak service took place well away from the church and Demyan could almost hear his mother's protesting screams as the coffin was lowered into unconsecrated ground.

Her final resting place would have been Annika's worst nightmare.

'Why didn't she tell me just how bad things were?' Katia asked as they walked away from the graveside.

'*Slishkom gorda,*' was Demyan's flat response as he turned and looked at his mother's grave. Yes, Annika Zukov had been too proud to ask for help from anyone and yet, Demyan thought bitterly, she had been too weak to change for herself or her son.

'Things will get better now,' Katia said, putting her arms around her nephew's shoulders, but Demyan shrugged her off.

They flew from a harsh St Petersburg winter into an Australian summer. Dark, sullen and quietly grieving, for most of the trip Demyan sat beside Katia, staring unseeing out of the small oval window, yet he was hauled from his dark thoughts by the majestic beauty of the land beneath. He had heard that Sydney had one of the most naturally beautiful harbours in the world.

Now he believed it.

For the first time in a very long time, what he had been told had proved right.

It was like seeing the sun for the first time. It hurt and blinded yet he could not help but look again. Demyan's heart was still ice, as cold and dark as the ground his mother now lay in, but in that moment, as he approached what was to be his new home, as he saw for the first time the Opera House and the Harbour Bridge, he swore never to return to Russia. He would take nothing for granted and he silently vowed that he would embrace each and every opportunity that this fresh start afforded him.

Demyan *had* embraced every opportunity.

Each and *every* one.

He had soon learnt to speak English, albeit it with a strong Russian accent. His understanding, though, was excellent, as were his grades. They remained so when he entered university. Study always came first but when he closed his books, when his work for the day was done, *then* Demyan indulged.

Few could resist his dark brooding looks and the occasional reward of that sullen face breaking into a smile. Sex was always on Demyan's terms, though; he didn't want to linger with kisses but what he lacked in affection he made up in skill, though he got bored easily and soon moved on.

Nadia was a brief fling.

A fellow Russian in Australia, it was nice to speak and hear his own language. His brain grew tired after half an hour of conversation in English.

It was just one night, except there were consequences and at nineteen Demyan found out he was about to become a father. He gave up studying and got a job. He was soon in demand, many companies wanting his sharp mind on their books, but even back then Demyan refused to commit to one company—he hadn't been able to control his mother's world but he was in complete control of his own.

His riches didn't come soon enough for Nadia and by the age of twenty-one Demyan was divorced, yet he didn't consider his brief marriage a failure for Roman, his son, was his finest achievement.

Had been.

As the wheels of his jet hit the tarmac Demyan closed his eyes and tried to block out Nadia's appalling revelation, yet he forced them open. He was here in Sydney to face things.

It was going to be a difficult visit. The press had found out that Nadia was marrying Vladimir and taking fourteen-year-old Roman to Russia to live.

The Zukovs were the equivalent of Australian royalty and the press did not want to lose this glamorous, fractured family and were goading Demyan with cruel questions that he steadfastly refused to answer.

Demyan was sped through customs and airport security did their best to shield him from the waiting press.

Perhaps they would have been better shielding the press from Demyan, for though he walked with seeming nonchalance and his head held high, behind dark glasses his eyes were scowling. If one more camera got in too close they would have an amazing shot for the late editions because with the mood Demyan was in he could have taken them all down with his hands tied. Demyan didn't even offer a sharp '*No comment*' to the questions about Nadia and Roman.

He had no desire to speak to the press when he couldn't even discuss it with his own son.

How, Demyan tried to fathom, could he possibly tell Roman that he might not be his?

Even thinking it had pain shoot, like neuralgia, through his brain.

'*Dobryy den,* Demyan.' Boris, his Sydney driver, wished him good afternoon, and as they left the pack behind and headed towards home, Demyan called Roman and again got no answer.

Finally, reluctantly, he called Nadia.

'I want to speak with Roman.'

'Roman's away with friends for a few days,' Nadia said. 'He wants to spend time with them before we leave for Russia.'

'No more games, Nadia. *I* want to spend time with him before he leaves. I am here in Sydney. You are to tell me where he is.'

'Why don't we meet and talk about it? I could come over...' Nadia's voice lowered and Demyan gave a black, mirthless smile into the phone. If Nadia only knew how cold her attempts at seduction left him, she'd surely save her breath. Less than a month before her wedding, it gave Demyan no pleasure that she would drop Vladimir in a moment.

Demyan could have his ex-wife in his bed tonight if he chose to.

He chose not.

'I have nothing that I wish to discuss with you.'

'Demyan—'

He terminated the call, if he hadn't, he might tell Nadia exactly what he thought of her and it wasn't in the least complimentary.

'Take me to a hotel,' Demyan instructed his driver, unable to face going to his penthouse.

It was no longer a home.

'Any preferences?' Boris checked, as Demyan stared out of the car window, watching as summer sped by.

'When does the new casino open?' Demyan asked.

'Not till next week.' Boris answered, suppressing a smile. Yes, Demyan was back in town! 'I assume you're invited?'

'Of course,' Demyan said, irritation scratching his throat, because the distraction of a brand-new hotel complex and high-rollers' casino was, in his current mood, rather tempting. 'Find a hotel where the presidential suite is free and will remain so for my duration in Australia. Probably a month.'

Marianna, his PA, was based in the United States and would normally deal with any sudden requests from her boss, but Demyan chose his staff carefully and all were versed in his ways, so Boris made a few calls and it wasn't long before they were pulling into the forecourt of a luxury hotel.

The staff fell over themselves to assist with the unexpected arrival of this most prestigious guest.

A teenage celebrity had that morning vacated the presidential suite and it had already been prepared for the next guest. However, that it was Demyan Zukov arriving ensured that as he swept through the foyer, twenty-four floors up, a multitude of staff were frantically doing their best to ensure that every detail was perfect for Demyan's sudden arrival.

The door was opened and Demyan stepped in and barely gave his surroundings a glance.

Hotels, however luxurious, were all pretty much the same.

'Can I get you anything?' the butler asked. 'A drink perhaps…'

'My privacy.'

'Would you like—?'

'I would like to be left alone. I will call if I need anything.'

As the door closed, for the first time since the news had hit, Demyan was properly alone.

For the first time since Nadia had revealed her foul news, he gave himself a moment to take it all in. He'd been denying there was even a possibility that Roman wasn't his son, of course. Roman had to be his. Demyan had held him the moment he'd been born, had looked into his son's eyes and felt love seep into his closed heart for the very first time and had never doubted that Roman was his child.

Demyan had attempted to suppress the news Nadia had imparted in a haze of alcohol and women.

It had almost worked.

It just wasn't working now.

Despite the hotel staff's best efforts, as Demyan sought distraction and flicked through the selection of newspapers, there was one detail they had missed—Demyan exhaled as he saw a magazine with both himself and Vladimir on the cover and the quirky question—*Who would you choose?*

They missed the point entirely, Demyan thought bitterly—Nadia had no choice, even if she occasionally embraced the fantasy that they would one day be a family again, he would never take her back.

Still, the tabloids loved to play their imaginary games. Demyan thumbed through the pages till he reached the article. There was Vladimir, early fifties, extremely wealthy with a stable reputation; the one thing missing in his life—a son.

Then there was Demyan.

Thirty-three, his vast wealth made even Vladimir look poor and his relative youth, combined with dark, brooding looks, meant that in the handsome, rich stakes, Demyan undeniably won hands down.

The negatives?

He didn't have to flick a page to find out what they were, but he did so anyway. Yes, he was a playboy, yes, he ricocheted across the globe, crashing in hotels, preferably with a casino attached. Yes, he disappeared at times to his luxury yacht and a selection of blondes.

Demyan worked hard and partied harder.

He was single—so why not?

As Demyan read on he saw that for once the press had almost played fair.

Yes, he had a scandalous reputation but that was tempered by his huge success and the fact no one could question that he was a good father and adored his son, and that his debauchery generally remained overseas rather than joining him when he returned to Australia.

Sydney was his base, his home, the rest of the globe his oyster.

But why wasn't he fighting Nadia? The article demanded.

Why was he letting Nadia take his son to Russia without putting up a fight? Whatever Demyan Zukov put his mind to he seemingly achieved, so why didn't he demand in the courts that his Australian-born son remain here?

Demyan read on, his gut churning at the questions and suppositions, especially knowing that Roman would surely be reading the same things.

The article was unrelenting. Perhaps Demyan didn't really care, maybe the father-and-son images had been all for the cameras? Was there a new Mrs Zukov waiting in the wings perhaps?

God help her if there was, the article said.

Was Demyan perhaps weary of the frequent trips to

Sydney and now only too happy to let Nadia fully take over the parenting of their son?

Demyan poured a drink and took a gulp and then walked to the window—not to take advantage of the view, more to torture himself with it.

From here he could see his penthouse—he was at eye level with it, in fact. Three stories of luxury yet it was the rooftop terrace that held his gaze now. So many evenings he had spent there with his son and his friends, listening to their God-awful band playing. It was there that Demyan had taught Roman to swim.

Demyan hurled the glass across the room in anger as he tore his eyes from his home.

He could not stand to set foot inside. He wanted it sold, he wanted it gone. There was also the farm in the Blue Mountains, his first home in Australia, that needed to be dealt with too. If Roman went to Russia then there was no reason for Demyan to be here. No reason to ever come back.

Demyan thought about calling his PA to join him here and deal with everything, but decided against it—though he liked her ordered, professionalism, in the bedroom she was getting far too clingy of late. Anyway, this wasn't business, this was personal. If this was to be his last trip to Sydney then a lot of things needed to be taken care of and, Demyan conceded to himself, it was going to hurt.

Demyan picked up the phone. 'I need an assistant for a couple of weeks, perhaps a month. Someone who is discreet and used to dealing with real estate.'

'Of course. When would you like—?'

Demyan interrupted the question; he rarely made small talk.

'Tomorrow morning at eight.'

Tomorrow he would deal with things.

Tomorrow he would start dismantling his life here and then leave it behind for ever.

There was nothing to hold him here any more.

Demyan headed for the decanter and filled a fresh glass.

What to do with himself this Wednesday night? He would hit another casino, Demyan decided. Tonight he would get blind drunk and, for once, his reputation would join him in Sydney.

Blonde, Demyan thought, inhaling the liquor.

No, brunette, or perhaps a redhead?

Why not all three?

Tonight he would party like tomorrow did not exist.

He took a drink and glanced once again towards the window, to a view that had once soothed him.

Just not today.

CHAPTER ONE

WHY HAD SHE LIED?

Alina Ritchie let out a long nervous breath as her taxi neared an incredibly sumptuous hotel.

Pulling her mirror out of her bag for perhaps the fifth time since the taxi had collected her from the apartment she shared with Cathy, she checked her appearance and wished *again* that, if she had one, her deeply buried sophisticated gene might today make itself known.

So far it hadn't.

Alina had put her toes through her one pair of stockings but thankfully they hadn't laddered and she had simply tucked the hole under her feet. Her carefully applied make-up had all but disappeared and even the short walk to the taxi had seen her pinned, long, dark hair start to coil and frizz in the humid, late-summer air. Alina set to work, taking the shine off her face with a brush and hopefully smoothing her hair with her embarrassingly damp palms.

Today *had* to go well, Alina told herself.

Even if she had only got this opportunity by default, it was the break that she had been waiting so long for.

Determined to forge a safe career and with her mother's somewhat bitter but terribly sage advice burning in her ears, Alina had put aside her interest in art and opted instead to study for a business degree. 'Ask yourself how many struggling artists there are, Alina,' her mother had said when, at the final hurdle of her application, Alina had wavered. All she had wanted to do was paint but her repertoire, as her mother had all too often pointed out, wasn't particularly vast.

Alina painted flowers.

Lots of them!

On canvas, silk, paper, and in their absence she painted them in her mind.

'You need a decent job,' Amanda Ritchie had warned. 'Every woman should have her own wage. I can't support you, Alina, and I hope I've brought you up to never rely on a man.'

Her mother's disenchantment, the fact Amanda was losing her small working flower farm had sealed Alina's fate—she'd opted for the corporate world but there were more than a few struggling PAs as well, and Alina was one of them. Work had been very thin on the ground and Alina's rather introverted, at times dreamy nature didn't fit in too well in the busy corporate world.

Alina's main source of income came from a restaurant where she waited tables four, sometimes five nights a week. Just before leaving for work last night she had taken a frantic call from a very exclusive agency that Alina had signed on with a few months ago. They rarely called her—Alina, with her rather round shape, didn't quite fit into their rigid square holes...

Until they were desperate!

Alina had blinked in surprise when she'd heard what they had in mind for her. A city hotel had called with an urgent request that a temporary PA position be filled for a very esteemed guest. None of the agency's preferred staff were available at such short notice, especially as the time frame was vague—a couple of weeks perhaps, possibly a month. Not wanting to pass such a plum opportunity to another agency, they had called Alina.

'Your résumé says that you have had some dealings in real estate?' Elizabeth, who had first interviewed Alina, had checked.

'I do.'

Alina hadn't exactly lied.

Rather, she just hadn't specified on her résumé that the sum total of her real estate experience had comprised of helping her mother sell the farm before the bank had foreclosed on it.

Then Elizabeth had told her that the client she would be working for was none other than Demyan Zukov.

'I take it that you do know who he is.'

You couldn't not know who Demyan Zukov was! He actually dined at times at the very elite restaurant where Alina worked, though their paths had never crossed. The last time he had been there she had been home, sick with tonsillitis, and on her return had had to suffer all the staff talking about the very glamorous guest.

Alina had been very tempted to confess there and then that this role was completely out of her league but the thought of having Demyan listed on the credentials part of her résumé had simply been too irresistible to pass up.

The agency had ensured the contracts and signatures were rushed through—Elizabeth had even turned up at the restaurant where Alina had been working that night to ensure that the deal was signed off.

'All our clients are important, Alina, but I hope I don't have to tell you just how important this one is.'

'Of course not,' Alina had said, but Elizabeth had been too worried to be subtle. 'Are you sure that you're up to this, Alina?'

'Absolutely.'

It hadn't helped that when she'd delivered her assured answer Alina could see the doubt evident in Elizabeth's eyes.

You are up to this, she told herself as she stepped out of the taxi and stood for a moment at the entrance to the hotel, trying to will herself calm, watching as elegant men and slim-suited beauties walked by confidently.

Yes, today had to go well because if it didn't...

Alina blew out a breath as she made a promise to herself.

If this didn't work out then she was going to quit even trying to survive the corporate world and just hands up admit that it wasn't for her.

If only she'd kept to her diet, Alina thought, feeling the bite of her waistband.

That was the problem with working at the very top-end restaurant at The Rocks—the owner was nice and ensured that all of the staff got a meal from the sumptuous menu on their break.

Who could say no to that?

Not Alina.

She was a country girl at heart and had an appetite to match, yet today she had to play the part of a slick city PA who allowed nothing to faze her.

Not even the formidable Demyan Zukov.

Alina could feel sweat on her top lip as she made herself known to Reception and was asked to show her ID.

'One moment, please.'

Oh, God, Alina thought, she wasn't even going to get past the receptionist! But a few moments later she returned and handed Alina a card for the elevator that would take her up to the presidential suite.

Alina actually felt sick as the elevator hurtled her towards the twenty-fourth floor. Worse, though, was when the elevator door opened at its destination and a very beautiful raven-haired, mascara-streaked woman stepped in as Alina stepped out.

That must have been his date for the night, Alina decided.

Alina had read more than her fair share of glossy magazines and so she was pretty well versed as to Demyan's rather decadent lifestyle.

Or she'd thought she was!

As Alina walked down the corridor a teary, pale blonde beauty teetered on high heels towards her. Alina could see, though she very quickly diverted her eyes, that the woman's left breast was exposed.

Nothing fazes you! Alina reminded herself for the hundredth time, though she was terribly tempted to simply turn tail and run.

Just act as if you've seen it all before, Alina told herself.

But she hadn't.

As she went to ring the doorbell to his suite her hand paused when the door opened and Alina swallowed nervously as she prepared herself to come face to face with the legend that was Demyan Zukov. Instead, it was a gorgeous redhead that stepped into Alina's line of vision, though the woman barely gave Alina a glance as she swept her way out of the master's chambers.

Alina was very used to being looked straight through.

Nondescript—she had actually heard Elizabeth describe her as that on the phone once.

It was an asset at times, Elizabeth had assured her as Alina had sat there with cheeks flaming. Some of their clients actually asked for the most nondescript women, Elizabeth had explained, so as not to inflame jealous wives.

Joy!

'Hello!' Alina knocked on the open door and waited. When there was no response she wondered if she should step inside or wait to be invited in. Her brief from the agency had stated that she was to arrive at eight.

Alina glanced at her phone—it was two minutes to.

'Hello!' Alina knocked and called out again. 'It's Alina Ritchie from the agency…'

Again there was no response.

Perhaps, given his busy night, he'd overslept, Alina thought, tentatively stepping inside.

The place was in utter chaos. There were clothes strewn everywhere as well as plates and glasses still wearing the evidence of having once been dressed with the most lavish food and drinks.

'Hello!' Alina said again, but then her panic mounted and she wondered if she was about to find him dead from his excesses in bed.

Stop it! she cursed her overactive imagination, but really, with all the evidence to hand and with all that she had read about Demyan, it was a distinct possibility.

She stood, trying to work out what she should do, but then she almost shot from her skin as a deep, richly accented voice came from behind her.

'Good, you are here.'

Alina swung around and braced herself—for what, she didn't really know but the sight that greeted her certainly wasn't on the list of possibilities that her mind had produced. Demyan might just as well have spent the night being groomed and pampered in the hotel spa to prepare for this moment. Like a beautiful phoenix rising from the ashes, he stood, looking absolutely exquisite, amidst the chaos.

The angels must have dressed him because his attire was the closest thing to perfection Alina had ever seen—an immaculate dark suit accentuated his tall, lean frame and his shirt was so white it was gleaming, but what drew Alina's eye wasn't just the dark silver-grey of his tie but that it matched his eyes, when first she met them, perfectly.

No, not perfectly, Alina, decided, because colours and hues were perhaps her favourite things.

Nothing could match his eyes—they made even the night sky seem dated. If he wasn't so imposing, Alina could have stared into them for ever.

'I'm Demyan.'

As if she needed to be told.

Alina took his outstretched hand and felt his long dry fingers close around hers. She caught a waft of his cologne, one that would surely mean her weekend was going to be spent in a perfume department just so that she could inhale that heady sent again—bold, clean and fresh yet with a musky undertone. She had never smelt anything quite so delicious before.

'I'm Alina.'

'Alina?' Demyan gave a small frown. 'That is a Slav name, no?'

'No,' Alina croaked. 'Celtic...' She could barely speak he was so stunning. Where was the crashing hangover he should be nursing? His black hair was freshly washed and brushed back and he was clean-shaven. Demyan's skin was smooth and pale—certainly he didn't come up all red and blotchy as Alina did if she drank so much as one glass of wine. On second brief inspection Alina saw that his dark eyes were perhaps a touch bloodshot but apart from that there was no evidence to denote a clearly wild night.

This was his usual, this was how he lived, Alina realised as she attempted to speak on. 'Actually, it can be both.'

'Both?' Demyan checked. He'd already lost the thread of the conversation and desperately needed the kick-start of a very strong coffee. Usually he did not leave his bed without one but, remembering that he had ordered the temporary PA to be here at eight, instead of having his coffee brought to him, Demyan had first showered and dressed for work.

Work always came first for him.

He had never once been late, or missed an appointment. Every facet of his life he controlled to the letter.

Demyan was not at the top of his game by either chance or mistake.

'I think it's both Slav and Celtic. It means...' Alina stopped herself then as she sensed his distraction. What would Demyan care about the meaning of her name? He had merely been making small talk. 'What can I do for you?' Alina asked instead.

'Coffee.' Demyan said. 'A lot of it. And could you also ask that someone comes to sort the place out?'

'Do you want breakfast as well?' Alina asked, heading for the phone to ring down for room service.

'I want coffee,' Demyan said, but halted her as she went to pick up the phone. 'Just press the bell in the butler's kitchen.' He frowned as she blushed and did as asked.

She couldn't even get an order as simple as coffee right but, though Alina had worked with a few overseas clients at hotels, she had never found herself in the presidential suite before, where a butler was just a bell press away.

'Could you organise coffee and for someone to come and sort out the suite?' Alina said, when the butler knocked and she opened the door. She bit back on her need to apologise for the terrible mess as the butler's eyes glimpsed the chaos behind her.

'Certainly.'

Demyan gestured to her to join him at a large walnut table, where he had pushed aside an empty bottle of cognac and several glasses and was opening up his laptop.

'I have allocated all of today to let you know what I expect from you in the coming weeks. I have two properties that I wish to sell…' Demyan hesitated. He had a vast property portfolio and most of his investments were purchased and sold unseen, but all of that took place away from Australia. The two properties that were about to go on the market here were far more personal. 'I want you to speak discreetly with some agents and give me the best two, perhaps three, and from there I will meet them and decide who to go with.'

'I'll ring a few this morning—'

'And say what?'

His tone was suddenly sharp and, looking over, Alina saw that his eyes had narrowed and she realised that she had clearly said the wrong thing.

'Firstly, you haven't even seen the properties. Secondly, you are to be discreet. The last thing I need is the press to find out before I tell…' Demyan hesitated again. He certainly wasn't going to discuss his predicament about Roman.

'You will make discreet enquiries with the agents, face to face, give me a shortlist, *then* I shall make my selection and *then* I will speak with them.' He was still frowning. 'You have done this type of thing before?' Demyan checked. 'Because I also have a farm out in the

Blue Mountains and it is going to be a complicated sale. I have tenants and they're not going to be particularly thrilled that I am selling. I do not need someone with no experience making—'

'Do they run their business from the farm?' Alina interrupted, blowing out a breath as Demyan gave a small nod, because there she did know what she was doing— her mother's farm had at one stage nearly been sold to overseas investors, which might have meant that her mother could have retained the business. Unfortunately, at the last minute the property had sold to a well-heeled family that wanted a place in the mountains as a weekender.

'I know a very good agribusiness agent,' Alina said. 'One who is very used to sitting tenants and international investors, though of course I'll liaise with others.'

He had been about to tell her to leave.

Even ordering something as simple as a coffee had proved complicated but, just as he was about to dismiss her, Demyan decided to give her another chance.

'You are a country girl?' Briefly he tried to understand her.

'Ex,' Alina said. 'Though you know what they say…'

'No,' Demyan said. 'They?'

'You can take the girl out of the country…' Her voice trailed off. 'It's a saying. You can—'

'I will call the tenants now.' Demyan cut her off in mid-sentence. He was possibly the most abrupt man she had ever met.

Alina watched as he effortlessly, and without so much as a flinch, broke the difficult news. 'I want to clear my portfolio here,' Demyan said, and Alina looked away; it was all just a little too close to home. 'I understand that, Ross,' Demyan said, 'but my decision has been made…'

Demyan stopped talking for a moment as Ross made rapid pleas. 'It will be going on the market as soon as possible.'

He just said it.

It *was* too close to home because Alina felt tears prick at the back of her eyes as she thought of Ross picking up the phone and how so much had just been dashed in one call.

Alina could hear Ross's voice rising, asking why Demyan couldn't have given them more notice, and then, for the first time, she heard a trace of emotion in Demyan's voice. 'I only decided last night.'

CHAPTER TWO

IT WAS A very long morning.

Alina sat embarrassed and uncomfortable as the staff worked around them, picking up the pieces of a decadent night.

Demyan didn't appear embarrassed, not remotely so. He was clearly more than used to it and they worked on solidly.

'Are there tenants in the other property?' Alina asked.

'No.' Demyan didn't even look over as he answered. 'It is my private residence that I am selling. Do you see now my need for discretion?'

Alina slowly nodded and ran a tongue over suddenly dry lips as she started to glimpse the enormity of Demyan's revelation. 'Am I to look for other—?'

'I am not buying,' Demyan said, and Alina blinked at the implication that he was leaving Australia. 'It is going to be a busy month—unexpectedly so.' He did look at her then—straight into her eyes. 'Do you have any questions?'

'No,' Alina said, hoping to make it clear that she wasn't about to pry, but again it was none too subtly pointed out that she was perhaps out of her league.

'Surely you should have many questions. You are supposed to be running my diary and arranging the sale of two properties and yet there is nothing that you wish to ask me? As I said earlier, I have allocated today to bring you up to…' His hand moved in a circle as he tried to place the word. Clearly irritated, his excellent English slipped and he repeated the start of the phrase. 'Bring you up to…'

Alina sat there, her lips tight, trying not to break in and give him the word that he was looking for. She didn't want to annoy him further—in fact, she was expecting any minute now to be told to leave. And then the strangest thing happened. She watched as his arrogant, sullen features slipped into a smile, the first she had glimpsed from him, and, most surprisingly of all, it was aimed at her.

'I don't have a stutter,' Demyan said.

Alina swallowed; she had no idea where this was leading.

'You don't have to just sit there and pretend not to notice that I cannot find the right word.' He was still smiling, just a little, but enough for Alina to realise why he so easily broke hearts. His smile was completely mesmerising. He had a very sensual mouth when it wasn't scowling, full, deep red lips that moved incredibly slowly, so slowly they made Alina aware that her own lips were itching and she ran her nail over them.

'Feel free to jump in,' Demyan said, and her thoughts were so lost in his lips that for a bizarre second Alina thought it was an invitation to kiss, but she quickly dragged her mind back to the conversation.

'Speed,' Alina croaked. 'You have today to bring me up to speed.'

'So use it wisely.'

Alina nodded.

'In the future if there is something you are unsure of, or you have questions—'

'Then I'll ask you.'

Wrong answer.

Alina knew because she actually saw his jaw clamp and that gorgeous mouth harden.

'If you would let me finish…' There was no trace of a smile on his lips now. 'I was about to say that you will liaise with Marianna, my regular PA in the States.'

'No matter the time of day?' Alina said. 'With the time difference…'

'You liaise with her before you trouble me.' Demyan said.

They worked on but not well.

'Ring Hassan's assistant,' Demyan said as the clock approached eleven. It had been the longest morning of her life and it didn't get any better. 'See if you can schedule dinner tomorrow. He is only here for a week, so make him a priority.' He had to pause before continuing because Alina wrote every instruction down. 'He likes a restaurant at The Rocks and I haven't eaten there in a while.' He circled his hand again and Alina hoped he was going to give a different restaurant name but, when it came, it was the one she worked at.

'Problem?' Demyan asked.

'No,' Alina answer too quickly. 'Why should there be?'

'Because you didn't write it down.'

He missed nothing, Alina realised, duly writing it down and waiting for the next set of instructions, but Demyan was silent now.

Alina was sure, quite sure, as lunchtime approached that Demyan had decided it was all too much hard work and that he might just as well send for the terribly efficient Marianna.

She was right.

Alina, Demyan had decided, wasn't a PA's shoelace. He had never met someone so excruciatingly shy and apologetic. She blushed whenever he spoke to her. Demyan was very used to women blushing but not quite so deeply and so consistently as Alina.

He actually called Marianna but, hearing the neediness in her voice, decided against summoning her. Maybe it was his pounding headache that made the thought of Marianna helping him deal with these painful transactions suddenly not appeal and he decided to give Alina a small period of grace.

Alina was ringing restaurants and contacting Hassan's PA when Demyan hung up on Marianna.

'Could you have some painkillers sent up?' Demyan said, but as Alina headed for the bell, he changed his mind. 'Actually, there are some in my bathroom, if you could fetch them for me, please.'

The staff had worked their magic and there was no hint that Demyan had entertained three women there last night.

That's what you're dealing with, Alina told herself, because, yes, she was attracted to him. In fact, she was more attracted to Demyan than she had ever been to anyone in her life. Not that he'd ever look at her in that way, Alina knew that, and she wasn't being modest. He was out of her world. So much so that Alina knew she shouldn't even be here. It had been terribly foolish to lie and even more foolish to tell Elizabeth that she was up to working for Demyan.

Alina stood in the palatial bathroom and forgot for a moment that she was in there for a reason as she admired his things. Oh, there was so much to admire—not a hint of plastic, Alina thought, looking at his heavy silver razor. There was nothing disposable about him. The diligent cleaners still hadn't quite managed to erase the scent of him. She couldn't help herself. Alina picked up a heavy crystal cologne bottle and held it in her palm, squinting to read the name.

Demyan.

He had his own fragrance.

Alina could barely take it in. She removed the glass stopper and inhaled deeply, the scent exactly him, heady, exotic, bold. She could have breathed it in for ever, but hearing his phone ring she jumped a little, knocking a little bit onto her face and hand.

Quickly Alina replaced the stopper and punched out two tablets from the packet then headed back out to where Demyan was on the phone. He was speaking in Russian and, from the less than pleasant tone he was using, and because he said Nadia's name, he was clearly talking to his ex-wife.

Alina stepped back into the bedroom and hovered, listening to her boss's simmering anger and hoping she could just get through today without it turning on her.

'Souka!' Demyan said, and Alina heard the clatter as he tossed the phone.

That's what you're dealing with, Alina reminded herself again, because, as her mother had always told her, you could tell a lot from a man by the way he spoke to or about his ex.

Yes, her toes might be curling in her shoes just looking at him but there was no doubt in Alina's mind that Demyan Zukov was an absolute bastard.

It was just that her body said otherwise.

Demyan glanced up as she approached. Those cheeks were on fire again but possibly, Demyan conceded, more from embarrassment at the disagreement she had just witnessed.

Demyan didn't need to explain himself and he certainly wasn't about to tell Alina what Nadia's response had been when he had called her a whore—instead of dissolving or crying, or better still hanging up, Nadia had simply dropped her voice and purred into the phone, *'If you want me to be.'*

Alina held out the tablets, watching his mouth lift into a very wry smile as she held out her hand.

'It will take a bit more than two,' Demyan said to her offering. 'Bring me the packet.' When Alina still stood there, he was more specific. 'Bring me the packet and a glass of iced water.'

'It says on the packet that the dose is two.' Alina watched his spiky black lashes blink at her small defiance.

'If I wanted a nurse I would have hired one.' His eyes lifted and met hers and Alina found that she was holding her breath as Demyan paused and his very straight nose breathed in air that was scented with the cologne she had spilled. 'A nurse who didn't meddle with my toiletries. Bring me the packet.'

'I'm not getting you any more.' Alina didn't care if it meant that she was fired—she certainly wasn't about to feed Demyan his drugs, even if it was just a couple of extra painkillers that he was asking for. She saw his eyes widen a touch, watched him open his mouth to speak, but Alina got in first. 'If you want to overdose then you can fetch them yourself.'

Alina put the tablets down on the table in front of him and waited for the same roar he had served Nadia.

It never came.

Alina blinked in surprise when Demyan merely shrugged and stood up, though he did not head to the bathroom to get any more tablets; instead, he picked up his jacket. 'We will go and look at my residence but first we will stop for lunch. Perhaps it is fresh air that I need more than painkillers.' He liked her shy smile and the way that her serious brown eyes flared in relief.

He liked it that she defied him.

So few did.

'Ring and book a table.' Demyan had made more decisions than he cared to this morning, he simply wanted lunch. 'You choose where.'

That should be it.

With anyone else, that would have been it.

His word, her command.

'Actually…' Alina gave a tentative cough before continuing, 'I can't have lunch with you.'

'Excuse me?'

'I have to have lunch separately from the client.' Alina attempted the impossible, to explain rules to a man who made his own. 'It's in the agency guidelines. It's on the contract that you signed last night.'

'Did I?'

Alina fished out the boilerplate contract from her bag and showed Demyan, who looked at his unmistakable signature. Last night remained a bit of a blur. 'So I did.' He flicked through the contract. 'It says here that you are to finish promptly at five, with no exceptions. Can I ask why?'

'I'm a temp,' Alina said. 'It's simply the agency guidelines.' She didn't add that Elizabeth would very possibly throttle her if she knew what was being said. Elizabeth would have her staying back to midnight if it pleased Demyan. Neither did she add the guidelines meant that by finishing promptly at five she was able to work in the evenings.

'Very well.' Demyan shrugged. 'We have a lot to do between now and five but first I need to eat.'

Alina called a restaurant from the list Marianna had emailed over and she called for his driver too, who was waiting for them as they stepped onto the forecourt.

For the first time in her life, Alina felt heads turn.

Though, of course, they turned for Demyan.

The door to a sleek silver car was being held open and after a teeny hesitation Alina realised that Demyan was waiting for her to get in.

In the back.

With him.

So this was how his PA lived, Alina thought as they drove through the city. With him, not beside him but separate, for she might as well not be there. At first he made no attempt at conversation, instead looking out the window, quite content not to fill the silence.

Alina's heart was still hammering; it hadn't stopped since they'd first met. It was close to one o'clock and almost five hours since first she had laid eyes on him and not by a flicker had his beauty or presence dimmed.

Alina stared out of her own window, unused to the awareness that had flooded her body, and then she heard his voice.

'Roman was born there.' He said it more to himself. Aware that his time in Australia was now limited, Demyan had been silently taking it all in. He stared at the hospital as they passed it, remembering how proud he had been that day, how determined he had been to do this right.

As Alina turned and glanced over, she noticed that all the arrogance in him seemed to have gone; she had never seen such sadness. Had she known him, even loosely, she would have followed instinct and asked what was wrong for there was torture in his eyes as they passed the hospital.

'So was I.'

Alina's voice and his mild surprise at her statement pulled Demyan from introspection and their eyes met. It was surely the only similarity they shared, Alina thought. Demyan's vast wealth would ensure now that he attended only the most esteemed private hospitals but that Roman had been born there told her that he had started from the bottom.

'How long ago?' Demyan asked, and she told him it had been twenty-four years.

'My mum wanted to have me at the local hospital or at home but I was complicated. I mean, the pregnancy was complicated.' She blushed. Alina always did around men and especially him, but this had more to do with what she had just said. She didn't usually open up easily and yet she just had.

'I would have been nine years old,' Demyan said. 'I don't think I had even heard of Australia then.'

Alina did the maths and placed him at thirty-three, and she knew from the glossies and a little internet research yesterday that Roman was fourteen. 'You were a very young father.'

'Not really,' Demyan, said and he didn't respond to her questioning frown. He wasn't about to explain to his PA that he had never in his life felt young. Even as a small child he had had so many responsibilities.

'I went to school near here.' Alina filled the silence.

'I thought you lived in the country.'

'I boarded during the week,' Alina said. She told him the name of the school and Demyan raised one eyebrow. It was a very strict, all-girls school. 'My mum was very adamant that I get a good education.'

'That's good.'

'Believe me, it wasn't.' She looked at two girls walking along, chatting, in red and white dresses and boaters. 'Even the sight of the uniform still makes me feel ill.'

'You didn't like high school?'

'I hated it,' Alina said. 'I didn't fit in.'

'That's not such a bad thing.' Demyan shrugged and got back to looking out the window but he didn't end the conversation. 'I never have.'

Alina looked over at him.

Wondered about him.

But Demyan had gone back to his own space.

They pulled up at the restaurant Alina had booked and she felt just a little bit foolish when she again declined his offer to join him for lunch.

'I'll meet you back at the car.'

'Very well. How long does the contract say you have for lunch?'

She knew he was being facetious. Demyan wasn't going to plan his schedule around her and she asked the driver to text her as soon as Demyan was ready to leave.

Yes, some might consider her foolish, for instead of joining Demyan and eating from the most luxurious menu, Alina bit, without much enthusiasm, into a salad sandwich that she had prepared that morning.

It felt far safer, though.

Alina had never met anyone so completely male before. She had never known her body react even remotely the way it was this morning and it scared her.

She blew out a long breath and gave up on her sandwich. There was a low, unfamiliar thrill at her very base that all morning she had been doing her level best to ignore. Now, instead of ignoring it, she tried reason.

Stunning to look at he may well be, but he was bad,

he was dangerous. The way he'd spoken to his ex-wife told her that, the three women leaving his suite were a pretty decent clue…

Alina took a less than enthusiastic bite of her apple and then promptly threw it in the bin.

She was sick of apples.

Alina headed for a vendor and ordered a hotdog.

'Extra onions, please,' Alina said. 'And extra cheese.'

She really had promised she would stick to her diet this week but a morning spent with Demyan and a hotdog, even with extra cheese, seemed a very mild vice to have.

He went against everything Alina liked in men, especially the way he behaved about his son. Yes, Alina had read the same magazine! How could she possibly even begin to fancy a man who could simply let go of his child? Well, Roman wasn't a child exactly, he was a teenager. She had only been three when her father had left.

Alina bit into the salty, greasy hotdog and for the first time since two minutes to eight her mind escaped Demyan. She looked up at the skyscrapers and the Sydney skyline, wondering if her father was behind one of the windows, working through his lunch break perhaps? Or maybe he was among the group of suited men walking towards her?

Would she recognise him if he was?

Would her father recognise her?

Would he even care? Alina thought, going to take a huge bite of her hotdog and realising she'd already finished the thing.

Obviously not.

Demyan had chosen to eat outside and sat on the terrace, idly watching the crowds go by, when he saw Alina throwing her apple and sandwich away and then buying the lunch that she clearly preferred—he had never seen someone eat a hotdog so fast!

Should he keep her or not? Demyan mildly pondered. Alina was nothing like Marianna or his regular staff, who were as efficient as they were unobtrusive.

He found himself frowning, because it didn't make sense. Yes, he might sleep with Marianna at times, but when working she could be sitting beside him and he wouldn't even notice. Alina was so shy and so eager to fade into the background that you actually couldn't help but notice that she was there.

So shy, so pleasing, yet she'd refused him those pain-killers.

'Can I get you anything, sir?' the ever-attentive waiter asked.

'Another coffee,' Demyan said, but as the waiter walked off Demyan called him back. 'Could you find me some painkillers? Just bring me the packet.'

'Of course, sir.'

That was better, Demyan thought briefly.

Actually, it wasn't.

He remembered the burn in her cheeks as she'd said no to him. Demyan looked back to where she stood, watching the world go by, and he found himself admiring her generous curves.

God, wouldn't it be nice to bed her? Demyan thought. Once she'd stopped apologising, once she had forgotten how to be shy. Wouldn't it be nice just to go back to the hotel room and get reacquainted with curves.

The richer he got the slimmer the pickings.

He would save her for later, Demyan decided. Alina would be a very nice reward to look forward to once he had faced the tough weeks ahead.

Demyan took time over his second coffee.
It had nothing to do with keeping her waiting.
He simply didn't want to go home.

CHAPTER THREE

THEY MET AT the car but Boris didn't open the door. Instead, he was speaking with Demyan, who had loosened his tie and was now wearing dark glasses. Demyan barely glanced over as she approached.

'We are walking,' he said as Alina went to open the car door.

Walking?

Where?

Demyan walked faster than Alina and she struggled to keep up.

'How far away do you live?' Alina asked, her feet already killing her.

'We are here.'

'Oh.'

Of course he'd be in the centre of everything.

A doorman greeted them and Alina held her breath as they stepped into a dark, blissfully cool foyer and approached the elevators.

'You will speak with Security and they will issue you with keys and a code, but for now use mine.'

Oh, Alina!

She wanted to borrow his dark glasses, she wanted to hide her fear because this was so far beyond anything she had imagined. He could almost *feel* her worry as they walked towards the entrance. 'What?' Demyan asked as he turned and saw her biting on her bottom lip. 'What is wrong?'

'Nothing,' Alina said, suddenly remembering the hole in her stockings. 'Do I have to take my shoes off?'

'Excuse me?'

'I forgot to bring flats,' she offered, but really she was more worried about the hole in her stocking and the fact it had been a little too long since she'd paid due attention to her toenails.

'Alina.' He turned and faced her before opening the door. 'Do I look like someone who would ask you to remove your shoes?'

'I don't know.'

'I'm offended.'

Alina looked up.

He wasn't offended.

Oh, she couldn't see his eyes behind his glasses, but his lips were smiling, just a little bit, and to Alina his mouth looked beautiful as he spoke on. 'And you don't look like a woman who carries flats, just in case,' Demyan said.

'I want to be one, though.' That smile was still almost there and Alina rewarded it with the truth. 'There's a hole in my stocking.'

Had he not still been wearing dark glasses, Demyan suspected that Alina's stockings would have promptly evaporated from the look he shot her, but he bit back a very wicked response to that comment, as he took out his key. He'd been dreading coming here and certainly hadn't expected to be smiling, let alone mildly turned on as he put the key to the door.

'How good are you with numbers?' Demyan asked, before opening the door.

'You mean maths?' Alina gave him a little *yikes* look. 'Awful!'

'I mean memory,' Demyan said, and then recited six numbers as he opened the door. 'Now punch them in.'

Alina had a very good memory.

Usually.

Except as they stepped into paradise she could smell him again and that feeling was back low, low in her stomach as he stood behind her. Demyan stared at her pink ears as she managed the first three numbers.

'I can't.'

'You can,' Demyan said, and she could feel his words reverberate down her spine. 'You have forty more seconds and if you get it wrong, or you are too late, the place will be swarming with security—'

'No pressure to get it right, then,' Alina interrupted. She could barely breathe. It wasn't the numbers that were the issue, it was their issuer. Alina doubted she could recite her two times tables with Demyan standing behind her. His hand was now hovering over hers and the thought of contact, the thought of possibly imploding at his touch... Somehow she punched them in.

'Good girl.'

His compliment she found curious, yet there was another shiver of thrill as she turned around, but Demyan had started walking.

'This is the one and only time I'll be here with you,' Demyan said, in business mode now and loathing being back. 'Any questions you have, speak up now.' Oh, she had plenty questions as she gazed around. There was a huge staircase in the middle that beckoned upwards, but for now Alina couldn't even begin to take that in. It wasn't just that there was a picture-postcard view, they were *in* the postcard, high, high above the Opera House, in the centre of a pulsing city, and Alina felt like a spinning needle in a compass, giddy as she stared out of the windows.

'Come on.' Demyan didn't give the view as much as a glance—instead, he gave her a brief tour.

'There are three floors as well as the garden terrace.' He just marched through his home, irritated when Alina lingered, but the vastness and luxury was simply all too much to take in.

'You can wander through later,' Demyan said, now desperate to get out. He didn't see the luxury, just the memories. He didn't see sumptuous lounges and polished tables, he just saw him and Roman sitting there, eating breakfast, planning their weekend. Demyan could barely stand the bar, for it was here he had hoped to celebrate Roman's eighteenth. Neither did he step in as he opened the door to the cinema, remembering birthdays when Roman had brought his friends.

It was choking him to be back.

He took the stairs; he just wanted out. Certainly he did not want to linger on the second floor.

'Why are you selling?' Alina swallowed. As she saw the rigid muscles in his face Alina explained her question. 'Isn't that what the vendor or buyer will ask?' His face was as black as thunder but it *was* the first question.

'"Reluctantly",' Demyan said. 'That is the word you use. It sounds as if I love it, that I'd rather not give it up, or it suggests financial hardship and that maybe they are getting a bargain. "Reluctantly" is a good word to use.'

'Okay.'

'I don't want to be caught up in the details.' Demyan explained. 'You are to be here with the chosen agent at all times. I will give you my figures and you will have my authority to decline.' Then Demyan thought of something. 'What if a prospective buyer wants to view the place on evenings or weekends—given that you must finish at five?'

'I'm sure we can come to an arrangement,' Alina answered.

It wasn't just luxurious, it was all so immaculate—until Demyan opened a door.

'Oh!' Alina smiled when she saw that, in contrast to the rest of the penthouse, one room did need attention. A lot of it. It was, despite the expensive finishings, still very much a teenage bedroom. There was a guitar and music sheets on the floor, cups, glasses and some wrappers.

'I'll make sure the staff have this cleaned,' Alina said.

'No.' Demyan halted Alina as she turned. 'Roman does not like the domestic staff in his room. He is supposed to keep it tidy by himself, though he hasn't been doing a very good job.'

'Well, if you're trying to sell it then it needs to be shown in its best light.'

'If a guitar on the floor and a few chewing-gum wrappers are going to dissuade anyone, then they are not serious about buying,' Demyan answered tartly, and then he paused. He was telling her to call in florists, designers, everything to show the home in the best possible light, yet he refused to have his son's room tidied. It was better perhaps to explain why properly.

'I don't know if Roman will be returning here before he goes to Russia. In my country it is considered bad luck to clean and tidy the room of a person who has left, until they arrive at their destination. It is only for Roman that I do it,' Demyan said, and then stopped even trying to explain it.

Alina nodded, though she didn't really understand.

Neither did Demyan, yet some of his mother's superstitions were still so ingrained that, though logic told him to ignore them, he simply could not take that chance.

Not with Roman.

Until he knew his son was safe at his destination the room would remain untouched.

They walked up another flight of stairs.

'The master bedroom,' Demyan said, though it needed no introduction. Alina could never have guessed that, apart from staff that cleaned it, or people like her, who were paid to deal with his busy life, a woman had so much as crossed the threshold.

Alina looked around. It was an incredibly masculine bedroom and it felt strange to be standing in here with such a very masculine man. 'You might want to think of a few feminine touches,' Alina suggested.

Demyan stopped in mid-yawn. He hadn't slept on the plane, or since he'd landed yesterday in Australia, and it was starting to catch up with him. The bed looked rather tempting.

So too did Alina.

He couldn't quite read her. She was curiously provocative, yet Demyan wasn't sure if she was being deliberately so.

'Some cushions or paintings…'

'Whatever you think,' Demyan said. 'Any more questions?'

'I don't think so.' Alina said. 'Or is that the wrong answer?'

'Not this time. I will speak with security and arrange keys.'

'Do I need a set for the agent?'

'No one is to come here unless you are present. Certainly they are not to have access to keys and security codes.'

It was a completely different world. There was no

popping out in your lunch break to get another set cut. Instead, the keys were all security coded and Alina had to sign for them and for an elevator pass as they made their way out.

'I have a lot of staff,' Demyan said when he saw her frown. 'I need to keep track of who has access.'

'I'm sure you have a lot of valuables.'

'I value my privacy.' He had no choice but to address it as they were met by his driver and got back into the car. 'Alina, you don't seem to understand my need for discretion.'

'I do.'

'No.' Demyan would not be placated. 'When you say things like, "Do I need a set for the agent?" it is clear to me that you do not understand. As soon as word gets out that I am selling my house there will be people trying to arrange to see it. This is the home I bought so that I could spend quality time with my son here, so I could be a proper father to him. I do not want it used as fodder to sell more magazines and I don't want tourists wandering through it either. Alina, are you quite sure that you know what you are doing here?'

His jaw gritted when Alina didn't answer. 'If you're not up to it, then have the guts to say so.' Demyan saw her rapid blink and his mind moved to make concessions, though he didn't really know why.

Perhaps he was being too harsh. It was the end of a very long day and she had seemed very confident about the farm.

'I am going back to the hotel. My driver will take you to speak with estate agents.'

The keys were burning in her hand.

'Have you managed to contact Hassan's assistant?' Demyan asked in the car on the way back to the hotel.

'I have.'

'So it's all organised for tomorrow?'

'There are no bookings available at your first preference.' She was just a little bit pink as she gave him the news or, rather, invented a tale. 'But I found a fabulous restaurant on The Quay.'

'Really?' Demyan frowned. He'd never once had trouble getting a reservation anywhere.

'There's a wedding on that night,' Alina hurriedly filled in. 'It's been booked out for months. They're hardly going to move a wedding…'

'They usually would,' Demyan said. Alina felt her throat squeeze tight. Demyan was right. *Had* there been a wedding, *had* she actually rung her work and explained that Demyan Zukov wanted to hold a business dinner there, they would have closed off the area upstairs, they would have moved the wedding outside, they would have done *anything* to accommodate such an esteemed guest.

Maybe he wouldn't mind her working at the restaurant, Alina mused, though that wasn't the entire issue now.

Demyan was right, she was in way over her head and, no, she didn't have the guts to tell him.

She heard him yawn and stretch. 'Boris shall take you to speak with agents. If I am not around when you get back, just go at five. How did you get to work this morning?'

'Taxi.'

'Boris will take you home and collect you.'

'I'd rather make my own way.'

'Whatever suits you. If you want to drive then use valet parking.' He saw her swallow, not just at the cost but at the thought of her tiny, filthy car being valet parked—she'd have to spend the night cleaning it before that happened. 'We'll go to the farm tomorrow or early next week.'

There would be no tomorrow.

'Demyan…' She turned around but Demyan didn't. He was checking his phone and simply ignored her till they were back at the hotel.

Alina's doubts about her suitability for the role were only compounded when she was blanked by two of the real estate agents that she attempted to discuss her boss's property with.

The third, though, did give her a brief hearing. Libby, the proprietor, gave Alina approximately two minutes of her time.

'My boss is looking to list his residence and I wanted to discuss your marketing strategies—'

'Who is your boss?'

'He'd rather I didn't give that information at this stage,' Alina flustered. It was another world and she didn't know the passwords to enter. 'It doesn't matter.'

'The location of his home?'

'If I told you that…'

'The price range?'

When Alina gave a ballpark figure, she expected Libby's eyes to widen and for her to show a sudden interest, but instead her lips twitched into a thinly disguised smile. Alina admitted it to herself fully then—she had absolutely no idea what she was doing. 'Thank you for speaking with me.'

'Here.' Libby went to a drawer and pulled out a thick glossy folder. Possibly she was just hedging her bets but at least she hadn't completely dismissed Alina. 'Of course, when we are talking in that price range, *everything* is negotiable.'

'I'll tell him.'

Again, Libby's lips twitched into a smile and Alina realised Libby was doing her best not to laugh. 'Please do.'

It was all incredibly humiliating and Alina was almost in tears by the time she got back to the hotel.

Demyan wasn't there, or possibly he was sleeping off last night's excesses in preparation to do it all again tonight because the door to his bedroom was closed.

Alina took out her contract and read it, especially the clause about a twenty-four-hour trial.

He was probably going to sack her anyway.

The right thing to do would be to ring Elizabeth but Alina was just too raw for the bitchiness and anger that would certainly ensue.

There was another reason, though, that had Alina choosing not to return tomorrow, one she quashed down and chose not to examine.

Yet.

Yes, she loathed confrontation, so much so that Alina opened the drawer of the bureau and took out the thick creamy hotel paper.

Dear Demyan,
I hope you had a nice rest.

I am very sorry but, as I'm sure you have worked out, I'm not suitable for this role.

It is not the agency's fault. I perhaps exaggerated my real estate experience to them, so please don't hold them accountable.
Alina.

Her hand was shaking as she signed her name and she left the note beside his computer, imagining his reaction when he read it.

He'd wasted an entire day.

Demyan Zukov, Alina was certain, wasn't going to be best pleased.

CHAPTER FOUR

Friday was wretched!

Alina spent the day waiting for the explosion to come from the bomb that she knew she had set off.

She knew, even though they had exchanged phone numbers, that Demyan wouldn't be the one to contact her. All day Alina waited for Elizabeth's caustic call.

The worst thing was, it never came.

No, the worst thing was the promise she'd made to herself if things didn't go well.

Alina pulled her paintings out of her wardrobe and some other artwork too, trying to pluck up the courage to make a booking for a stall, but when she heard how much it would cost she didn't follow through.

Yes, it was a wretched day and a portion of it was spent hiding behind her laptop.

She didn't look Demyan up, instead she tortured herself with another name.

Her father's.

Alina did this fairly regularly but always, till now, it had been to no avail, but there her father was on the screen of her laptop, smiling back at her, his wife and three daughters beside him.

Two years ago Alina had tried to find him but had gotten nowhere.

Now, with her mother overseas, Alina's need to make contact with her father had increased and at last something about him had appeared online.

It *was* him.

Alina stared into dark brown eyes that matched hers.

Kind eyes, she hoped as her fingers hovered over the keyboard. She wasn't asking for support, or to blaze into his life, Alina told herself.

She was merely asking to be his friend.

Alina heard the door open as Cathy, her flatmate, popped home on her lunch break and Alina hurriedly hit send.

'Oh!' Cathy was there with her boyfriend and clearly a bit put out that they didn't have the place to themselves. 'I thought you had a month's work lined up.'

Alina hadn't told her that she would be working for Demyan—Cathy wasn't exactly discreet.

'It didn't work out.'

'That's a shame. Cheer up, something else will come along.'

Not from the agency, Alina thought, picking up the house phone and ringing her mobile just to make sure that it was working. She couldn't believe that Elizabeth hadn't called.

'Will you get paid for yesterday?'

'I doubt it.' Alina more than doubted it.

'Well, at least you've still got the restaurant. Are you there tonight?'

Alina nodded and then held her breath, knowing what was coming next.

'I might have a few friends over when you get back. Just letting you know.'

Great!

It would be more than a few people. Cathy had parties

all the time and Alina was desperate for a place of her own and was frantically saving towards that goal. Sydney prices, though, were terribly expensive.

Perhaps she should have just faked it with Demyan for a little while longer, Alina thought as the sound of Cathy and her boyfriend having sex filled the small apartment.

Demyan.

She wondered just how cross he was.

Worse, she wondered if he'd even deign to note her leaving with a shrug.

He was still there in her mind that evening as she was getting ready for work.

She pulled on her black skirt and T-shirt and loosely tied back her hair. There was no hope of make-up staying on in a busy restaurant so Alina didn't bother with it. The restaurant, though exclusive, had a casual ambience and the waitressing staff were all young and friendly. Most of them were students, all of them, actually…

Except Alina.

Alina pulled on her sandals and headed for her shift. She took the bus as parking in the city was far too expensive.

Sydney was beautiful but never more so than now. European royalty was visiting and the new hotel and casino were opening soon and the place throbbed with excitement. Tonight the restaurant would be crammed to bursting with the beautiful and well heeled.

Before starting her shift, Alina checked her phone, wondering if her father had made contact yet.

Still no.

'Cheer up, Alina!' Pierre, the manager, said as he briefed the evening staff on the house specials and dishes of the day. He wasn't being kind, he was telling her. 'Our guests don't need to know that the waitress is having trouble with her love life.'

Love life? Pierre couldn't know but that was a rather black joke and there, an hour and a day after she'd written Demyan that note, Alina knew the real reason she'd walked out on the opportunity of a lifetime.

Demyan.

The man himself.

Yes, Alina loathed confrontation and she'd never known a man as confronting as him.

As sexually confronting as him, Alina amended as she pushed out a smile and got on with her evening.

Clearing a table around nine, her mind was so conflicted she wanted to just sit down and put her head in her hands to get it straight.

Yes, she was naïve and might have acted as if she'd seen it all before yesterday morning when those women had left...

She just didn't want to see it all again.

'Alina!' She could hear Pierre calling to her as she came to a painful truth.

She was already jealous of whoever Demyan was bedding.

It had had little to do with work.

'Alina!' Pierre came over. 'Leave that and get table four ready.' Table four was the best one and already taken. Alina glanced over and saw an extremely put-out couple walking past. 'I had to move them—Zukov is coming here.'

Alina felt the colour drain from her face.

'Demyan Zukov?' She had this brief surge of hope that it might be Nadia, she had been here a couple of times for lunch after all, but even before Pierre answered, the smile on his face told Alina the bad news.

'None other.' Pierre grinned. 'Oh, my God, he's here!'

'Pierre…' Alina started, but what could she say? That she didn't want to wait at his table? Pierre would simply tell her that she was fired there and then. Pierre was probably going to fire her soon anyway when he found out that she had lied and told Demyan that there was a wedding on.

The restaurant fell silent for a second as guests realised just who had entered and then there followed a buzz of excitement.

'This is Alina,' Pierre introduced them, 'and she will be looking after you this evening, as will Glynn, our wine waiter.' Alina saw Pierre frown at her less-than-effusive response so she quickly plastered on a smile, though she felt as if she were about to wet her pants.

'Alina.' Demyan frowned and repeated their very first conversation. 'That is a Slav name, no?'

She simply couldn't answer.

Instead, Demyan did. 'Or is it Celtic?' he mused, as he took his seat.

'Both,' Alina croaked. She was nearly in tears but still frantically smiling.

'Thank you for accommodating us.' Demyan turned to Pierre. 'I know that you are exceptionally busy tonight.'

'We're never too busy for you, Demyan.' Pierre blushed, as he gushed, as he flirted shamelessly. 'Any time.'

Any time at all.

'Thank you.' Demyan turned his attention back to Alina, who then had to go through her spiel about the menu.

'What would you recommend?'

He's enjoying this, Alina realised.

Demyan was.

At first, he hadn't recognised her. He'd been far too busy admiring a bottom and tanned, freckled, rather heavy legs, and then Alina had turned around and he'd realised they belonged to her.

His missing-in-action PA.

Poor baby!

That had been his first thought, yet, rather than put her at ease, teasing Alina was the most fun he had had in…

Ages.

'The lobster in lemon butter sauce—' she started.

'No,' Demyan interrupted. 'I think I'll go for tenderloin.'

She heard that word so many times a night; not once did it make her burn, never had it made her loins feel tender.

Till tonight.

Still, Demyan was a very good host and turned his attention to his guest, though he did tease her a couple of times during service. 'What happened to the wedding?' he asked when she brought the main course, and Demyan glanced at his empty water glass for her to fill it.

'They cancelled.'

'Liar,' Demyan responded softly, watching her shaking hand overfill his glass. He said it so that only Alina could hear and she turned her burning face to him.

'I'm so sorry.'

'I will deal with you later,' Demyan said, except he was smiling and so too, for a very brief second, was she.

Her first genuine smile of the night and Alina didn't know why, didn't understand the message in his eyes, for, had Hassan not been there, he might have told her that he would put her over his knee.

Alina thought herself as clueless at flirting as she was at temping.

She was doing it, though.

She knew exactly the moment his eyes were on her, even with her back to him. She could feel it, that was all.

And when she stretched her back, when she put her hands behind her waist and her bust jutted out a touch, even if it was without deliberate intention, it was for him. Her body, rather than her mind, seemed to know how to play this game.

It was a dangerous game, though. She knew that. But on what should have been the worst night of an already wretched day, for reasons she couldn't quite fathom, Alina felt like laughing.

Until he left.

Glynn had done everything he could to tempt him with dessert wine or cognac but to everyone in the restaurant's disappointment, all too soon, though respectably late, Demyan and his guest left.

'Off to cause mayhem,' Pierre sighed, swiping the wallet containing his tip before Alina could and then watching Demyan's suited shoulders depart.

Alina was beyond confused.

He hadn't told her off, he hadn't even seemed offended or slighted.

As they all huddled together at the end of the night, waiting for Pierre to put them out of their misery and tell them how big his tip had been, Alina's mind wasn't on the money—instead it was replaying Demyan's words. *I will deal with you later.*

It wasn't so much what he'd said, more the way that he'd said it, that had brought a flurry of unfamiliar nerves.

'Did you smell him?' Pierre asked, handing over their envelopes.

'No,' Alina lied, because she wanted to bathe in a scent named Demyan and then went very pink when Pierre gave out the divided-up tips and she realised how generous Demyan's tip had been.

He wasn't cross.

It was so warm that Alina hadn't brought a jacket. She grabbed her bag and though usually she walked quickly to get her bus, tonight she lingered a little, looking at the beautiful Opera House, when usually she dashed past, just enjoying the vibe of a warm Sydney night.

For once she was going to be reckless, Alina decided. Instead of adding the tip to her savings she was going to put the deposit down for a market stall.

For her, that was wild.

She wasn't petrified of blowing the money, she was just petrified of revealing her work and the appalling vision of no one caring to stop.

She was going to do it, though, she decided. Tonight he had made her feel just a little bit wild.

'Hey.' A hand tapped her shoulder and Alina's first instinct was to walk faster, not because she was scared of a stranger, this was no stranger to her brain for she knew Demyan's voice, would never forget it, yet instinct told her to run from him. 'Alina!' He caught her wrist and turned her around and the scent that had driven Pierre crazy was doing the same to her now. Yes, she wanted to run, for he was more than her senses could deal with.

'I have to get my bus.'

'You're *so* not getting a bus.'

'I'm sorry about yesterday.'

'First-day nerves.' Demyan shrugged. 'I'm very used to them. I will see you on Monday.'

'No.' It wasn't selling the penthouse that terrified her—it was him, it was the way that he made her feel.

'I'll drive you home.'

'The answer will still be no.'

'I won't ask again,' Demyan said. 'I loathe nagging.'

'Begging,' Alina corrected.

'I don't beg,' Demyan said.

Nag still wasn't the right word. Didn't nagging mean constantly pushing for something the other didn't want?

No, he wasn't nagging, she was simply too scared to say yes.

'Maybe we could go to my hotel and discuss it.'

'No!'

Oh, my God, Alina thought, he said it so easily. She tried to tear her mind from sex to the conversation in hand but they matched perfectly anyway. 'Demyan, I can't work for you. I don't have any experience.'

'I think you will do very well.' Demyan said. He was speaking the truth as he looked into brown, caring eyes. Those eyes were the reason that he had not fired her and why he had not called the agency today. It was *not* a nameless transaction. Selling up was difficult and Demyan had soon realised that Alina would take the care that the memories of his home deserved. 'Anything you're not sure of you will speak with Marianna. If she's a bitch to you, tell her I said not to be.'

'Why didn't you tell the agency I'd walked out?' Alina couldn't help but ask him.

'No need to. I was always going to ring you tomorrow. I thought I'd give you today to calm down. It didn't work, though, did it?' Alina stared into his beautiful eyes now in a way she hadn't been able to yesterday as his hand brushed hers and then took hold. His breath was on her cheek as energy thrummed in the lessening space between them. 'I'm not calm either,' Demyan said, and his hand toyed with hers a little and she almost wanted him to move her palm, her fingers digging into his as she resisted an urge, an urge that had never, till now, existed.

She wanted to feel him, *wanted* his hand to guide hers to his groin, and Alina had never known such a feeling.

She was breathing too fast yet it felt not enough.

'Your name means bright and beautiful.' Demyan saw her confused blink and he was just a touch surprised too at his own admission that he had looked her name up.

'It means light,' Alina said.

'Not where I come from.'

He watched her free hand move and her nails run across her mouth, as they had yesterday.

And he smiled as he had before, for they had wanted each other even then.

'If your lips itch, it means you will be kissed soon.'

'It doesn't.'

'Where I come from it does.'

'They don't itch.'

'Are you a compulsive liar, Alina?'

'They don't itch.'

They didn't any more—they burnt. She could feel the heat from his skin on her cheek, she could actually *feel* his words coming from the mouth she was now impatient to meet. She moaned in relief as his mouth ceased taunting and it was sublime. A few fumbled kisses and gropes was the sum of Alina's experience. This, though, was far from fumbled, his directness was heaven. His lips were soft and warm as they pulsed on hers then there was the delicious first brush of his tongue—warmer than summer; she shivered like winter and Alina never wanted it to end.

Demyan had been waiting long and hard for this but her kiss was as unexpected as his attraction to her.

God, it was nice, he thought, sinking in.

Wet but nice.

He tried to slow her tongue down with his, yet she

didn't read his dance. He could feel the utter inexperience in every clumsy stroke, yet it was so curiously nice.

So nice that his hand was stroking her thick nipple and wanting more of the same, even as his mind registered that there would be no spanky-spanky.

What the hell was he doing, necking in the street with a virgin?

Please, no!

He didn't have the time, or inclination, to take his time.

But, yes, she was a virgin, he was sure of it as his tongue firmly held hers still.

She felt the pin of muscle in her mouth and her tongue desisted then more slowly curled back to life against his.

She was so willing and pleasing, an A-plus student, in fact, for her kiss was one a usually bored by now Demyan wanted. His fingers were in her T-shirt and as he peeled back her bra and his thumb grazed her nipple again he felt the moan in her throat. It was pleasing to feel her purr into sexual life, so completely rewarding that he wanted to play a little bit more, yet Demyan resisted.

He liked her.

Maybe more than he cared to admit, but while he wanted to linger and continue this delicious perusal, while he wanted that mouth trained by his, he attempted to slow things down. Yet she was harder to get off than red wine on a white rug. His mouth kept going back to hers, swirling in ever-decreasing circles, wondering if he might just give her one come, wondering if he might... wondering what the hell...

'Come on,' Demyan said, peeling his mouth back, holding her hips. 'My driver will take you home.'

He saw the flare of disappointment in her eyes as he retracted the hotel offer.

Her body was warm and he stared at her all flushed and aroused and he was tempted to put scruples on ice as, bold now, she made her move.

'We could go back to the hotel.' Oh, my God, Alina couldn't believe *she'd* just said it, but she had, she *had* and she meant every word.

'Alina,' Demyan cut in—he could be very blunt when he needed to be. 'I'm not going to be here for long.'

'I know that.'

'I shall be leaving Australia soon and I have no intention of ever coming back.'

Okay, a little too direct at times but it was necessary because he could see the wrestle in her eyes as she made peace with that.

'I get that.'

'Alina, I'm not someone that you should be cutting your teeth on.' He saw her blush when she didn't need to. He was simply telling her the truth, he was bad, he had no soul and he never looked back. 'Back to business on Monday.'

He walked her to the car and although usually he'd walk off, this time he actually climbed in.

'You are not to let me out of this car,' Demyan said in Russian to Boris. 'My order is to make sure she gets safely home. Alone.'

'What did you say to him?'

'To avert his eyes.'

He forgot he loathed kissing and Alina forgot her own address as he kissed her all the way home. Indecent kisses and not just from Demyan, her mouth telling his what she wanted now.

'You,' Demyan said to her as Boris tapped on the window, 'are amazing, and way too good for me.'

He turned it all around, he turned her whole word around.

'You're having a party?' He frowned at the music.

'My flatmate's having a party.'

It offered them an excuse to go back to the hotel.

He resisted.

'Bed,' Demyan said. 'Alone and safe from this wolf. Consider it forgotten by Monday.'

She'd *never* forget.

Alina stepped in and closed the door. She was a little high from a very nice kiss, a little confused from a very unexpected night, and then, as she headed to the relative quiet of her room and checked her phone to see if her father had made contact…

…more than a little devastated.

CHAPTER FIVE

DEMYAN WASN'T IN the best of moods on Monday because he still could not get hold of Roman.

Nadia blocked his attempts to meet with his son at every turn.

'Did you meet with the estate agents?' Demyan asked Alina.

'Just one,' Alina said.

'One?'

'I didn't get past the receptionists with the others.' Demyan held in a very irritated sigh. Why hadn't she just insisted?

'What did the one you did see say?'

'She gave me a brochure and said that at the prices I was discussing everything was negotiable.' Alina looked at him and he could see her blotchy, swollen eyes and he was arrogant enough to assume that he was the cause of them.

He wanted to get up from his desk and shake her and tell her not to wear her heart on her sleeve.

Give that girl a shot of confidence, he felt like shouting to the bar, except it was just the two of them here and it didn't make proper sense, because she'd had plenty of confidence the other night.

No. Demyan refused to think about the other night.

'I think Libby, the agent, thought I was a bit mad,' Alina said, and he tried not to smile. 'That you were my imaginary boss.'

'Call her,' Demyan said. 'On speaker.'

Alina did so and she could picture Libby's tight smile when she was put through.

'Ah, Alina, how are you?'

'Very well,' Alina said. 'My boss has a few more questions.'

'Such as?'

It was Demyan who answered. 'How many clients you have on your books that would be looking in that price range.'

There was a very long pause. 'Several?'

'How many?'

'Two, possibly three, though that's before I put out feelers.'

'Names?' Demyan said.

'Not at this stage.'

'One name,' Demyan pushed, and there was a long hesitation.

'Not at this stage.'

'Alina will call you back.' He clicked off the phone.

Alina did call her back but not till five o'clock, and Libby answered her phone on first ring. When Alina confirmed that, yes, she was speaking about Demyan Zukov she suddenly found herself with a new best friend, and the next afternoon she showed Libby around the penthouse and they discussed what they could do to enhance perfection.

Alina was loving this part. Being a PA had been more her mother's vision than hers. She was never going to make much selling her artwork, but it felt good to be using that part of her brain again—working with colours, adding details that possibly didn't matter but which to Alina mattered a lot.

As for Roman's room…

'God!' Libby came up behind her. 'Did the cleaners miss this?'

'It's to stay like that.' Alina borrowed Demyan's words. 'If a guitar on the floor and a few chewing-gum wrappers are going to dissuade anyone, then they are not serious about buying.'

'Can I bring someone through on Saturday?'

'Someone?'

Even Alina blinked when Libby said a very famous couple's name. 'They're in Australia now but only till Sunday.'

'I'll check,' Alina said.

The door to Demyan's bedroom was closed when she returned to the hotel and, glancing at her phone, Alina realised she had missed a text from him, telling her to book him in to see his dentist tomorrow.

She wanted to knock so badly.

More than that, she wanted to go in and it had nothing to do with finding out his dentist of choice!

Instead, she called Marianna. It was the early hours of the morning in the States.

'I'm so sorry.'

'Why?' Marianna said, because she was far more used to Demyan's strange world than Alina was.

'I'm to book Demyan in for the dentist tomorrow. He just didn't specify which one.'

Marianna actually laughed. 'Of course he didn't.'

It was the most ridiculous conversation of her life but Demyan had meant what he'd said that first day and did not want to be bothered with minor details.

'Dr Emerson.' Marianna gave her the number, not the

number of the receptionist but Dr Emerson's number. 'Oh, and Demyan will want to be seen at eight a.m.'

'Thanks.' Alina called the number and got voicemail, and she smiled just a little to herself as she wielded some of Demyan's power. 'This is Demyan's PA, Alina. I'd like to make an appointment for him tomorrow at eight— a.m.,' she added, because Demyan could no doubt have both. 'If you can confirm, that would be great.'

He called to confirm two minutes later and Alina sent Demyan an email to bring him up to speed before she went home, though she'd have loved to linger.

She wanted to be behind that bedroom door and loathed that tonight someone else might be.

She could not stand that thought.

Demyan woke close to midnight.

His mind was black.

He felt like ringing Nadia or his lawyer and demanding to know the location of his son.

If he was his son.

Demyan dragged in air, but it did not calm him.

He picked up the phone to call Nadia, but what purpose would that serve? Maybe he should just go around there, but wouldn't Nadia just love that.

She was probably half hoping for it, baiting him to do just that.

Sex with your ex or a night in a cell for breaking her door down? Your choice, Demyan.

He might head to a casino.

He walked out to pour a drink and checked his email and saw, amongst many, that there was one from Alina.

He opened hers first.

I hope you had a nice rest.

Demyan found himself smiling and then raised his eyes as he read on because it would seem he had European royalty visiting his house at the weekend.

Go, Alina!

Libby agrees that the main bedroom is too masculine. I have a large watercolour painting that would look very nice on the main wall opposite your bed. It is too big for my apartment and lives in the wardrobe. I'll bring it in tomorrow, but please don't worry if you don't like it, I shan't be offended in the least. The colours are nice, that's all...

Demyan blinked as he read on—it was a *magnum opus* of an email.

I was thinking about Roman's bedroom. Again, please don't be offended, I might not be being very sensitive or politically correct. Why don't I take a photo of it with my phone, tidy it up and then put it all back, exactly as it was?

I have made you an appointment for the dentist tomorrow at eight a.m.!

Demyan didn't understand the exclamation mark and was pondering it as he replied.

Saturday is fine for the inspection.
I don't need to see the painting—whatever you think.
As for Roman's room...

Demyan hesitated, just sat there for a very long moment and then resumed writing.

...I am not offended at your suggestion. However, my mother said that if you touched the room before the other reached their destination, planes would fall from the sky, the earth would crack open and disaster would be wreaked so it is probably better to leave it as is. Demyan.

Instead of the casino he headed for bed and lay there for a very long time, remembering the confusion of his childhood and the terrifying rituals his mother kept changing while insisting that they were adhered to. There could be no empty bottles on the table, no half-filled glasses were allowed either...

Just an endless circle of rituals, and for what? It had changed nothing anyway.

His mother had ended up in hell.

He got up and sent a further email, now, before he changed his mind. It was ridiculous to be selling his home and not tidying the bedroom.

Alina, do whatever you think best with Roman's bedroom.

Then he lay on the bed and thought about her and wondered if she'd think it strange to get two conflicting emails.

Tough, Demyan thought, heading back to the computer, she was going to get three.

Just don't tell me if you do.
PS Why didn't you like high school?

CHAPTER SIX

'THERE WERE GOOD times, Demyan.'

Just back from the dentist, Demyan hadn't even taken his jacket off and he closed his eyes to Nadia's voice and then opened them to Alina, who was pretending to concentrate on something—though it didn't matter anyway as they were speaking in Russian. 'I can't remember any,' Demyan said.

He glanced at his computer and read the email Alina had sent him.

Okay, I will sort out the paintings and a few cushions and things.
Alina
PS I was always hungry.

It was sweet, unlike the buzzing of Nadia in his ear, and the dentist's anaesthetic was starting to wear off.

'Demyan,' Nadia persisted

'What the hell do you want?'

'Our family together.'

'Given what you told me, I don't know if I have one.'

'Demyan, please, I just said that in an argument.'

'No, because I don't argue with you, Nadia. And the

reason I don't argue is because I don't care about you enough to enter a debate.'

'Please, just think about it. I'm not asking for for ever. I just want us together...'

His head hurt from speaking in Russian, when it used to be the other way round.

As he terminated the call, Alina blinked.

She'd learnt a couple of Russian swear words working with Demyan. He glanced over at her pink cheeks.

This time it didn't sit right with him that she had heard that. There was a part of him that wanted to explain, except, he reminded himself, he chose not to explain himself to anyone.

Yet when Alina got up and headed to the butler's kitchen he could still feel her displeasure so he sent her a text.

You shouldn't have had to hear that.

He headed to his room, closed the door and lay on the bed and waited for her text.

Perhaps you're saying sorry to the wrong person?

No, Demyan texted back.

I am not sorry for what I said. The first text was correct.

He closed his eyes, again waiting for her response, planning his.

Getting hard.

God, but he loved the chase. He picked up his phone; she still hadn't answered him.

Alina was, in fact, speaking with Marianna. Now the world knew Demyan was in Sydney the invitations were coming in thick and fast and Marianna and Alina were going through them.

'Demyan still hasn't given a response to the new casino for their opening night. They really want him, especially now that they know he's here. Just prompt him.'

'I will,' Alina said.

They actually worked quite well together. Marianna had taken one look at Alina on a video call and decided there was nothing to worry about, and Alina had taken one look at Marianna and wanted to be her.

'This one it's probably best to run by him before turning it down,' Marianna said, and Alina blinked.

'A mental health–awareness charity dinner?' That was one Alina would have ticked no to. 'I didn't realise Demyan supported—'

'Royalty are attending,' Marianna broke in. 'The guest list is like a who's who .'

Of course, Alina reminded herself as Marianna continued, it would be about networking, her boss didn't have a social conscience.

'I declined for him a couple of months ago, explaining he wouldn't be in Australia at that time, but, of course, they've heard that he's back and are only too eager to have him attend. It's tonight.'

'I'll tell him as soon as he gets up,' Alina said before saying goodbye. 'Oh, and I'm sorry for calling so late about the dentist.'

'As I said, no problem.'

'Why doesn't he call the bloody dentist himself?' Alina grumbled, assuming Demyan was still in his room, and Marianna laughed and signed off.

'Ah, so it was a passive-aggressive exclamation mark.'

Demyan's voice from behind her had Alina nearly shoot out of her skin.

'It was,' she admitted, and there was no choice but to laugh.

'If I had the time to do things like book the dentist...'

'I know, I know.' Alina put her hands up. 'Then I wouldn't have a job. How was it, by the way?'

'Why do people even ask how the dentist was?' Demyan scowled. 'I'm going to bed.'

With Demyan back in his room Alina took a few minutes to search for her father's profile again.

Since Friday night she hadn't been able to find it.

Maybe her father was just overwhelmed, Alina told herself.

Perhaps he hadn't even got her request; maybe he'd just decided to take his profile down and she had nothing to do with it?

Alina glanced over at Demyan's computer, a small swallow in her throat as she wondered if she dared. She listened at his door for a moment and was soothed by the sound of silence.

She simply had to know.

Alina went to his desk and clicked on an icon. All she had to do was type in her father's name and—

'Alina!' Demyan's voice made her jump and she scurried to hide the page.

'I'm just...'

'Just what?'

Her face was purple, her eyes shining with terror, and, instead of being cross, Demyan was actually bemused. He even tried to ease her horror with a joke.

'If you want some decent porn then I am sorry to disappoint. I like it on the big screen at home...'

She was almost in tears, Demyan realised. In fact, she was actually crying and desperately trying not to. 'What were you…?' he tapped in for browsing history and gave a small shrug when a social networking site came up. Demyan really only used it to check on feedback about his hotels but he knew how it worked all the same.

'I tried to contact someone and I can't find their profile on my computer or phone…' Her voice was shaking. 'I'm so sorry. I wanted to see if they came up on yours.'

'Did they?'

'Yes.'

'So.' He shrugged. 'Someone blocked you. Don't take it so personally, I block people all the time. And,' he warned as Alina went to sit at her desk, 'don't snoop on my computer again. You could have just asked,' Demyan said. 'We could have had a play…' He hesitated, reminded himself she was off limits, but when he sat down, curious, he clicked on the page and all joking stopped for another reason entirely.

Poor baby! The thought came to him again as he stared at a man who, not just by his surname, was surely related to Alina, and definitely old enough to be her father.

A curious bastard, Demyan sent him a friend request and then looked over to where Alina was frantically trying to pretend she was working.

'Did Marianna have anything for me?'

'She did,' Alina said, her voice still shaken, and he merely yawned as she told him about the casino invitation.

'Maybe…' Demyan said. He was still cross with them for not being open last week!

'No way,' he said, when she told him about the mental health awareness function tonight.

Alina told him who'd be attending.

'No way,' Demyan said, but this time with a Russian swear word between the other two words. 'They'll be looking through my home at the weekend, the last thing I want is a close-up of my prospective buyers.' He paused, not pleased with himself for revealing that the sale was hurting him.

A small bleep alerted him and he glanced at his computer. It would appear he had a new friend.

Alina's father!

Bastard, Demyan thought, not quite sure why he was meddling, or even interested. He had no idea how he'd use this, just a certain knowledge that he would.

Demyan loved mind games.

'Reply and say…' He looked at Alina and then back at her father and hesitated. Maybe she deserved some fun. A small smile spread on his lips, a smile Alina had never seen—it could perhaps be labelled mischievous.

'Tell them that I would be thrilled to support such a worthy cause…'

'Really?' Alina couldn't make out his smile. 'I never thought of you as getting behind mental health awareness.'

'You should try co-parenting with Nadia.'

Now she got the smile.

'Tell them that we'll be delighted to attend.'

'We.' Alina frowned. 'You and…'

'You.'

'But I'm working…'

'For me,' Demyan said. 'Sort it.'

'Demyan, I—'

'Don't bore me with details, Alina. And if you wave that contract at me, I tear it up; if you choose to be working at the restaurant this evening, I fire you. Tonight, no doubt, they will want a speech as well as a donation

and there will be invitations too. My PA attends functions such as this one so that I don't have to remember
all that's said.' He glanced over. 'You can meet me back
here at six or I will pick you up.'

'But, Demyan—'

'Go.'

'It's midday.'

'I'm not that much of a bastard, Alina. I assume you
have to do your hair and sort out what to wear...' He leant
back in his chair and put his feet on the desk and made
up his mind. 'I will pick you up at six.'

'I...' She didn't get to finish.

'Be ready or don't bother coming back tomorrow.'

He said the sweetest things at times!

As she went to get her bag Demyan halted her.

'Alina.' He looked as she turned. 'I send you home
to get ready, not cry over some loser who blocked you.'

Yes, he said the sweetest things sometimes and this
time she meant that thought.

'I'll try.'

'Fifteen minutes,' Demyan said.

'Sorry?'

'Set a timer and give yourself fifteen minutes to cry
over him then get on with your life.'

'Is that what you do?'

'I don't have to get over people,' Demyan said. 'I don't
care for anyone enough.'

'You say the sweetest things.' This time she voiced
it.

This time he smiled.

Fifteen minutes!

It would take more than that to get over her father's
rejection. Alina fell through the door and onto her bed
and let her pillow have it, but actually, thanks to Demy-

an's surprise invitation, she didn't have time to bemoan her father.

What to wear to an A-list function?

I don't have anything suitable…

Alina started the text and then halted. Was she asking him for money, making excuses?

Demyan would see it as both.

Alina deleted the text and lay on her bed. The problem, though, was a real one, there would be serious money there tonight. Her work wardrobe consisted of suits and a rather large little black dress that she used for any work functions, and even if she hit the shops the type of dress she could afford simply wasn't going to make the grade and she couldn't afford designer…

Alina swallowed as a thought came to mind but though she pushed it away it kept building, so much so that she climbed out of her bed, went to her wardrobe and pulled out a box, telling herself that she was being ridiculous to even consider it. As she pulled back the tissue paper and pulled out the dress, it was even more beautiful than Alina remembered. Reds, purples and yellows pulsed beneath her fingers.

Her scattered mind had once flitted to, instead of paintings, designing and making dresses. She loved working on silk, loved the halo effect around the flowers, and she was lost in them now as she eyed her masterpiece.

It had taken many goes and she'd spent a fortune but, rather than doing anything with it, Alina had simply been unable to part with it and had spent another small fortune having it made into a dress.

'Stunning fabric,' the dressmaker had said, and Alina

had nodded, omitting to mention that the stunning fabric had been created by her own hands.

Was it stunning enough, though? Alina thought, eyeing herself in the mirror.

It was all she had.

So, instead of buying a dress that would still be deemed too cheap, Alina spent that money on having her hair glossed and expertly curled.

Oh, and on buying shoes!

Kissed-by-Demyan-Zukov shoes, Alina decided to name them as she tried them on.

She was *entitled* to celebrate that!

They were so beautiful that they deserved only the prettiest feet and so Alina spent what time she had left giving herself a pedicure, then a manicure, and finally she turned to her face. What was the point? She was always blushing around Demyan so it would only come off and yet, with him, she was no longer shy. Alina pondered that as she did her face, settling for waterproof mascara and neutral lipstick, and then imagined his mouth kissing it off.

She *was* going to sleep with him. She *wanted* to sleep with him. If her heart couldn't cope with being one of Demyan's flings then it had just better toughen the hell up.

As she stared in the mirror, and the knock on the door finally came, the very last thing on Alina's mind was work.

Demyan was expecting a black dress and a whole load of support underwear as he knocked at her door.

Good.

He was annoyed with himself now about asking her to accompany him. Still, it would serve well to remind Alina that his appalling reputation was merited, given that since she'd started working for him, things had been terribly tame. Well, no more! This was business, and sometimes he mixed it with pleasure. If he saw someone he liked, and he usually did, Demyan had every intention of Alina being driven home alone.

Then she opened her door.

A blaze of colour and curls and curves greeted him and it went straight to his groin.

Demyan didn't say the first thing that came to mind, it would have been far too rude, so he said the second—he told her she looked beautiful but in a way she could never understand. *'Tiy viy-gli-dish' kra-see-va.'*

'Swearing again, Demyan?'

'No.' He smiled. 'I was expecting black.'

'Black's for work.' Alina smiled. 'I'd never choose it, I like colour and light.'

'Come on.'

She smelt of summer and nervous energy and there was anticipation there too.

'When we arrive, do I—?'

'*I* arrive,' Demyan said. 'You will go in separately. I am a single man, Alina. You don't want to ruin my chances, now, do you?'

Alina swallowed. Nothing could ruin his chances but it was a very deft reminder that this wasn't a date, even if she'd somehow, by the time she'd painted her third toenail, convinced herself that it was.

It hurt far more than it should.

Alina was dropped off and showed her pass and was let in as Demyan drove around to where the celebrities and important guests were making an entrance.

He was completely at ease arriving alone, it was often one in, two out—he never left empty-handed. Then he saw Alina, standing there in that amazing dress, and he could see by the set of her shoulders he'd offended her, and when he took a glass of champagne and held one out to her she declined.

'Have one.'

'I'd better not, I'm working,' Alina said, and he laughed.

Yes, he'd offended her. Not arriving with him, shouldn't have, of course, this was high-end stuff and naturally he needed staff around him.

The royals arrived and Demyan turned his back at the first opportunity. He did not want to think of them in his home, did not want that picture in his mind.

'Let's go through.'

They were seated at a circular table and a terribly beautiful, very jittery blonde called Livia—'Not Olivia, Livia,' she corrected before anyone could make a mistake—visibly sagged when she saw Alina. Still, she perked up considerably when Alina was introduced as his PA.

'You're working late,' Livia said, and then got straight back to flirting with Demyan.

All through the meal she persisted, dismissing Alina as if she wasn't there, and again Demyan was very conscious that Alina was next to him. If it had been Marianna, even though they slept together at times, he'd be flirting back with Livia.

'I recognise her,' Alina said, when Livia excused herself to go to the loo.

Demyan recognised her too. Oh, not for her acting skills, he'd recognised the offer that had just been delivered—the slight tilt to Livia's head as she'd stood.

'I don't,' Demyan said, and turned and gave Alina a smile as the lights dimmed. 'Wake me up when it's my turn to speak.'

God, they droned on, Demyan thought. He loathed speeches and how everyone had to be thanked five hundred times when surely an email would suffice. Livia was back, more jittery than ever, and Demyan was just about to doze off when the voice on the stage reached him.

'I remember going to a friend's house for dinner and not wanting to leave. My friend and I fell out a few weeks later because I never asked her back to mine. I couldn't. I never knew what I might find and I also didn't want anyone else to see what went on at home.'

Demyan felt as if the spotlight was on him as this woman, this stranger, described, almost to the letter, his childhood.

He glanced at Alina, who was listening, with no idea of the chaos taking place in the head beside hers. He half expected a flash mob to stand and dance around him, because surely this was a set-up, surely this was *his* hell that was being so eloquently described.

Alina felt the tension beside her and turned and saw Demyan's intent expression as he took in the words.

'I did everything she told me, I did everything right, while knowing that I was setting myself up for disaster. If it worked, if we survived the night by tapping the bed four times before I got in, as well as taping the curtains together, as well as...' She gave a smile. 'I'm sure you get the message, but if it worked it meant we had to do it again the next time and the next and the next. The rituals became more complicated...'

Whatever Olivia was offering was becoming increasingly tempting.

Livia.

He was about to get up to walk off but he felt the calm of Alina beside him, laughing at a joke the speaker made. Then he found out that it wasn't his life being described, because the speaker's mother had got better at times and when she'd got worse, carers had stepped in.

He glanced at Olivia and didn't even correct her name to himself as she gave him a bored eye-roll. Demyan didn't give one back; instead, he listened.

He was truly shaken to his core.

'Her speech…' Demyan said to Alina as the applause started, then halted. He wasn't going to discuss this with his PA, he didn't need to explain things to Alina.

'Good luck,' Alina said, as Demyan got up to speak.

She watched intently. It was bliss to be able to examine him from a distance.

She watched as he went for his jacket and then changed his mind.

Demyan thanked everyone, very nicely.

The little barb about Nadia remained on the notes in his pocket and instead he spoke about how he rarely attended fundraisers, yet this was a worthy one and this charity he would do all he could to support.

'We hope that means Demyan will be back next year,' the MC said as Demyan returned to his seat, and as he caught Alina's eye, he saw her biting down on her lip, because she knew he was leaving Australia.

'Come.'

Alina didn't want to dance, or rather she did but the conflicting messages from Demyan were messing with her head.

He hadn't meant to dance either. Livia was making fervent glassy eyes and usually that would be the preferred option but, right now, he chose to inhale summer and he led Alina to the floor.

'Making promises you can't keep,' she said.

'I keep all my promises,' Demyan said. 'There is internet banking, Alina. I will give good donations'

'You know full well that they want more than your money.'

Demyan knew that, he was supposed to be closing things down, unjoining the dots, not putting his hand up.

'Are you still cross?' Demyan asked, trying to change the subject.

'About being dropped off at the servants' entrance?' She stared right back at him. 'It's a bit *Upstairs, Downstairs*,' she said, referring to a television drama set in Edwardian London.

He just frowned.

'Yes, Mrs Bridges,' Alina said to his frown.

'I haven't a clue what you're talking about.'

'You'd laugh if you did.'

Alina wasn't laughing as he pulled her in closer.

'Relax,' Demyan said.

But she was scared to, for if she did, for even a second, her hands might reveal that they wanted him closer, or her face might lift to his, so instead she danced rigidly in his arms.

'Why so tense?' he asked.

'I'm not used to functions like this,' Alina said, but did not explain that neither was she used to being in the arms of someone as incredible as him. Despite her bravery as she'd got ready, he'd made sure she'd got that message that this was work as he'd dropped her at the employees' entrance. She was trying for professional now but her body happily forgave that humiliation as her nipples throbbed beneath her silk dress and the tops of her thighs ached for attention from the man she kept half at arm's length.

The woman who had made the speech danced past them with her partner and Demyan wanted to tap her on the shoulder, to ask how, how did she stand there and admit things like that, how did she now dance and smile and laugh? Instead, he pulled Alina in closer and felt her resistance, and he held her there, his mouth to her ear as if to hush her protests.

Yes, she protested, but silently and only for a moment, her body tense at first but then she came to terms with the male dragging her deeper in. And then she accepted, leaning into him, and Demyan exhaled at the small compliance, his hand, moving a little lower than her waist.

He rarely danced, perhaps one, and then bed.

Dancing was boring, but now he wasn't bored.

They danced, because if they didn't the night ended, if they went back to their seats or took a drink or stopped then it ended, and Demyan didn't want to end it just yet.

He told her again she looked beautiful but he confused her again because it was in Russian.

'What does *"tiy viy..."*?' she couldn't remember the rest.

'It means you need sticking plasters over your nipples,' Demyan lied, but he could feel the mouth near his cheek stretch into a smile.

'Only when you're around.'

God, he was hard and this dark horse didn't mind in the least—she'd even made a small joke.

'You're working me too hard.'

'What happened to shy?'

'I don't know,' Alina admitted.

He was used to eager women but that wasn't the word he'd used for Alina.

Willing.

Not that word either, Demyan thought as his hand slid over her silk-clad bottom and his face moved in front of hers. 'What does malleable mean exactly?'

'Flexible,' Alina said.

'No,' Demyan said, as a vision that wouldn't help matters flicked into his head.

'Impressionable?' Alina offered.

'No…' Demyan shook his head. With two languages at his disposal he couldn't place the word he'd use to describe her.

'Persuadable?' Alina smiled.

That would be me, Demyan thought, because right now he could scrub 'no virgins' out of his rule book and bed her and bed her and bed her.

Beddable.

That was the word.

Breakable.

He looked at that lovely face and a mouth waiting to be kissed and he denied them both the pleasure, but for once it was for her sake.

'Come on,' Demyan said. 'I take you home.'

She didn't want home, she wanted back to the hotel, she wanted all his body had promised as they'd danced. The music shifted and they could step back but they danced one more dance and he moved them so they were well in the shadows. He wanted to kiss her, which was unusual for Demyan. She wanted a night with this man. In high heels she still didn't match his height but as she spoke, her mouth grazed his neck and she felt the pressure of his palm on her head and her lips brushed the skin, which wasn't a kiss and he could perhaps allow that.

His skin was not his mouth, but she kissed it as if it was and Demyan closed his eyes at the unexpected pleasure of her tongue on his skin and then the hush of his thoughts, for right now the only place he was on a dance floor. Right now, when he needed to focus more than ever, for a fleeting moment his mind wavered from its controlled path, and it jolted Demyan enough to halt her.

'Come on.' He was terribly nice to her because, to make things a little better perhaps, on the way home, he cared enough to lie. 'I don't get involved with people I work with.'

'Sure.'

Alina knew he was lying. Marianna had alluded to a couple of the perks of her job.

Demyan could be very blunt at times, but what he didn't know was that he should have been just a little bit blunter then. Had he simply said, *I don't do virgins,* Alina might have understood better.

As it was, she walked into her flatmate's noisy party, barricaded herself in her bedroom and then promptly burst into tears. She'd thrown herself at him. In her very best dress, in her Kissed-by-Demyan shoes, she'd thrown herself at him but, worse than that, Demyan, who'd screw anything, had turned her down.

He simply didn't want her, Alina realised.

No one ever had.

CHAPTER SEVEN

DEMYAN ASSUMED, though correctly this time, that Alina's red eyes were over him.

It was claustrophobic in the office, though the tension wasn't all down to last night.

Demyan went to his room and tried to call Roman but got sent straight to voicemail.

Nadia texted to say she was moving things forward.

She was now planning for her and Roman to leave as early as next week and so, Demyan decided, would he. 'Come now.' He strode out of his bedroom. 'We go and look at the farm.'

'I'll call your driver.'

'Just call for the car,' Demyan said. He was agitated, restless about the news from Nadia and also not in the least happy with his handling of Alina last night. The speeches were still playing in his head and her red, puffy eyes weren't helping matters. 'I'll drive.' As he went to put on his jacket he glanced down at her heels. 'Did you remember your flats this time?' Even as he said it, Demyan regretted the small tease. There would be no more mixed messages.

He just wasn't prepared for her answer.

'It's fine,' Alina said. 'I've got some boots in my car, I'll go down and get them.'

That was the woman she was, Demyan thought.

The trouble was, though, that he liked it.

As they left the city, Alina couldn't help filling the silence.

'I'd never have imagined you owning a farm. It's just not the sort of property I'd picture you having...'

Demyan shrugged. 'It is...' He tried to think of the best way to describe it. 'The constant toothache...'

'Farms are.'

'Always there is something to be done. If not the tenants needing something then there are boundaries or fences...' He shook his head. 'I should have sold it ages ago.'

'Why didn't you?'

Demyan was trying to keep it business on the two-hour drive there.

It *was* business, he had to remind himself as he told Alina what she needed to know.

'This couple were friends of my aunt's,' Demyan said. 'They had the neighbouring orchards. The property was left to me on Katia's death. I was never going to live there...' Alina glanced over, at his brief hesitation. 'Well, I did consider it at one time. Then there were bush fires and Ross and Mary's property and orchards were razed. I leased to them the house and my orchards. It has been twelve years. Their orchards are back...' Demyan drove through the mountains, trying to ignore his own disquiet.

'What about their home?'

'They chose not to rebuild.' He glanced over and saw her tight lips. 'They can make an offer. They have a very successful business, flourishing orchards...' He glanced over again. 'You're not writing it down.'

'I don't need to.' Alina looked out of the window. 'Our farm was described as flourishing too.'

'What produce?'

'Waratah.' She knew from the silence he was waiting for her to explain. 'They're huge, red flowers, beautiful, like a big cabbage…' Her voice trailed off. What would he care? 'I just know farming's hard. Selling produce is hard.' Alina gave a tight smile. 'Anyway…'

They drove the rest of the way in silence.

Business, Demyan told himself as he shook Ross's hand.

Ross had calmed down since the phone call. Demyan had been good to them after all. No, they wouldn't be making an offer, Ross said as Alina pulled on very well-worn leather ankle boots and they walked around.

This Christmas especially hadn't been a great one and Demyan knew from his aunt that when you sold cherries in Australia for a livelihood you lived and died by Christmas.

It was just as hard as expected to be back at the property where he had spent those years with his aunt, years spent thawing just a little from a brutal life.

It was harder, though, than he'd imagined, a couple of hours of discussions later, to be back in the house, to wash his hands in the bathroom and catch sight of himself in a mirror and see a man staring back instead of a mistrusting youth.

'We'll do this as seamlessly as possible.' Demyan said as he shook Ross's hand. 'Alina will be in contact and…' His voice broke off. For once Demyan didn't know how to conclude a business meeting.

'Of course,' Ross finished.

'I made you some lunch.' Mary's eyes were as swollen as Alina's had been that morning. 'I know it must be hard for you too, Demyan. I remember when you first came here…' She gave a soft laugh. 'Look at you now.'

'Times change.'

'They do,' Mary said. She offered him the basket of food. 'I thought you might want to take a last look around.'

Demyan didn't want one last look. He wanted to get into the car and drive off, to just drive away and never look back. To blow up the life he had built here because without Roman it meant nothing anyway.

Didn't it?

'Thank you.'

It would be rude to refuse, Demyan told himself.

Not that that had ever stopped him in his life.

They walked for ages, right up to the back orchards, and they walked in silence. Alina's head felt as if it was exploding. There was so much about Demyan she loathed—the way he spoke to his ex-wife, that he wasn't fighting for his son, that he was ripping up Ross and Mary's lives when surely, *surely* they must mean something to him.

Clearly they didn't.

She wanted to loathe him and yet...

Her world had never felt...

She had never *felt* as much as she felt now, walking through an orchard with Demyan beside her.

Alina felt like crying, like singing, like getting naked. She just felt.

'Do you want to take your lunch by that tree and I take the one here?' Demyan said, teasing her about the agency rules. 'Or you can eat in the car.'

'Stop.'

'I used to go there,' he said, pointing to a huge willow, its branches bathing in the river. 'It's much cooler.'

He held the green curtain open for her and she entered his heaven.

'I used to come here to think,' Demyan said, though he didn't tell her about what. 'We will have dessert first.' He took some scones and butter and cream and then smeared thick cherry jam on as Alina's mouth watered. 'I don't believe in saving the best to last.'

He handed the scone to her and watched as she took a bite.

'Good?' he checked.

'Amazing!'

'Why were you hungry at high school?' Demyan asked. 'Was the food bad?'

'The food was fantastic,' Alina said. 'But when you're a big girl you really wear it if you go up for seconds.'

'So you didn't go up?'

'No. It wasn't worth the bitching from the other girls.'

'I'd have told them—' Demyan started, and Alina interrupted him

'Mne pohuj,' Alina said, and she was rewarded by a brief burst of deep laughter as she told him, in Russian, what she should have said to those bitchy girls—that she didn't care a jot, only rather more rudely. Yes, she'd picked up a few Russian swear words, being around Demyan.

'More emphasis on the *po,*' Demyan said.

'Your language is terrible.' Alina smiled.

'My language is excellent,' Demyan said. 'In Russia swearing is an art.' He looked at her as she happily ate another scone. 'Say it again.'

'Nope,' Alina said. 'I'll practise in private.'

'Did you like growing up on the farm?' Demyan asked.

'I loved it.'

'Do you have brothers or sisters?'

'No.'

'Your mother?'

'She's overseas, having some "me time".' Alina rolled her eyes. 'She's earned it apparently, raising me alone.'

'Your father?' Demyan fished.

Alina shrugged. 'He left when I was three.'

'Do you see him?'

'No.' The sting of rejection from her father burnt so badly. 'Apparently he always wanted a working farm—that's how Mum and he met, she was a florist… Anyway, I came along and he decided it was all too much and just walked out on it. Mum tried to keep it going and she did well for a few years but it was tough on her, getting up in the middle of the night for the flower markets…' Alina shook her head. If she carried on talking about it she'd start to cry.

'So why did you decide to be a PA?'

'Because it's a much more reliable way to make a living. Businesspeople will always need assistants…'

It wasn't his place to tell her she was terrible at it.

Actually, it *was* his place.

Were it not for a very nice kiss, she'd have been fired. In fact, had he not been so hungover he'd probably have fired her the moment he'd realised she hadn't a clue about real estate.

He hadn't fired her, though. Perhaps because his skin didn't crawl when he thought about her walking through his home, his things.

He'd even allowed her to tidy Roman's room.

Demyan wondered if she had.

'Do you get a lot of work through the agency?'

'Some,' Alina said, then admitted the truth. 'Not an awful lot. I'm very grateful for my waitressing job.' She took another bite of her scone rather than explain to a man who would never get it anyway how much safer she felt knowing her half of the rent was covered, that even if she didn't get any work she had a meal at the restaurant four nights a week.

Had she told him, though, she might have found out that Demyan did, in fact, understand perfectly well.

'Do you enjoy it?'

'It's a very nice restaurant, the staff are great…'

'I was talking about being an assistant.'

Alina swallowed. 'Of course.' She flashed what she hoped was her corporate smile.

'Alina…'

She stared back at him.

I hate it.

How could she say that?

How could she say to her temporary boss that for the most part she loathed her job? Oh, she tried to make the best of it, yet she was careering badly down a path that she had never really thought through stepping on; she was just too scared to follow the path that beckoned more loudly.

No, she couldn't say that and so she turned the conversation to him.

'This is where you first lived when you came to Australia?'

Demyan nodded. 'My aunt ran it. She died when Roman was two.' Alina swallowed. So rarely did he mention his son. 'In fact, Katia died two days after my divorce was finalised. Nadia thought I should sell it but, given we were officially divorced, I told her…' He paused and they shared a teeny smile as he contained his language. 'That I did not care what she thought.'

'That's better!'

'I suggested she live here but Nadia wanted the city. In the end I rented it out.' He looked at Alina. 'Suddenly I had equity.'

'Your start?'

Demyan nodded.

'Did you ever think of living here?'

'Briefly.' Demyan shrugged. 'It was never really the same, though, once Katia had died. I thought of keeping it for Roman but…' Demyan shrugged. 'It seems he will be living in Russia.'

He could not go there; instead, Alina did.

'Will you travel to Russia to see him?'

'Of course,' Demyan said, even though he felt ill at the thought. He had always sworn he would never go back. 'I haven't lost him.'

Alina frowned at his choice of word but then told herself that Demyan's words were not always the correct ones. 'Of course not.'

Demyan hadn't even discussed this with his lawyer yet; he was precariously close to telling her, to admitting to what was killing him.

Yet he could tell no one.

Not even Roman.

Especially not Roman.

Demyan replayed Nadia's words.

'Please, just think about it. I'm not asking for for ever I just want us together…'

Nadia didn't love him, she loved the glamour, the name, the money, and when Roman turned eighteen, that money would dry up.

Another loveless marriage?

Demyan thought about it.

Another expensive divorce?

Demyan thought about that too.

It wasn't in the least palatable but if it meant that he kept the status quo—the life he had built, the times with his son in the country he had, for all these years, called home…

Checkmate.

Nadia had practically called it.

No.

He looked at Alina again. 'Have you ever been in a serious relationship?' He watched as her cheeks turned pink.

'Not really,' Alina said, then looked at him. 'Not at all.'

'Can I ask why?'

'I don't know,' Alina admitted. 'I knew that my dad had slept with half the village mums, I was always terrified there might be half-brothers that I didn't know about, so that was rather offputting…'

'Alina!' Demyan gave a shocked laugh. 'When you forget to be shy you are funny.'

'I know,' Alina said. 'I make myself laugh all the time.'

'Why haven't you slept with anyone?' He was deliberately more specific.

'I don't really know…' How could she best explain it? 'I'm not really into muscly, brawny guys, which is a shame because the pale, interesting men aren't really…' she looked at him. 'What sort of a man do you think I should cut my teeth on?'

Demyan would prefer not to think about her with other men.

He lay on his back in their little green glade and tried to picture the ideal guy for Alina's first.

He just couldn't.

Or rather he could, but the image in his mind came with his face on.

He looked at her brown eyes and round face and imagined some sleaze giving her too much to drink, or someone awkward and shy who would simply make her more awkward and shy.

'I was divorced with a five-year-old by the time I was your age,' Demyan said.

'I know.' She was quiet for a very long moment. 'Why did you two…?' No one asked, no one ever had, but she was either foolish or brave enough to ask. 'Why did you and Nadia break up?'

'I wasn't doing well enough,' Demyan said, then hesitated. That wasn't strictly true but he discussed it with no one, not even himself. Alina sat fiddling with the salt rather than look at him but her hand slipped and salt spilled on the blanket. Demyan felt the familiar clench to his throat and tried to ignore it. It was illogical to think that something as simple as spilling salt could cause disaster, but even all these years later he could hear his mother's wailing and screaming, the slap to his cheek for a simple accident. He frowned as Alina took a pinch and threw it over her left shoulder.

'What are you doing?'

'You know…' She gave a shy, embarrassed smile. 'It's bad luck to spill salt.'

'And that counteracts it?'

'It's supposed to.' She watched as he sat up and took some salt and went to throw it over his shoulder.

'The left one,' Alina said. 'That's where the devil sits.'

He looked into her eyes, saw her smiling face and the calm of her voice and the ice that had gripped him thawed just a little.

'My mother was very superstitious,' Demyan said.

'Oh.'

Alina took a bite of her scone.

'Very,' Demyan said, and watched as she looked at him. He had never really spoken of it with anyone. That note to

Alina had been the first time he had shared such a detail. Nadia had had no idea. She had laughed at the old superstitions and had happily placed an empty wine bottle on the table, and Demyan had long ago taught himself not to react, not to show weakness. 'That speaker last night, I thought for a moment that we must share the same mother.'

'I'm sorry,' Alina said, and then blushed because she was talking with her mouth full. She quickly swallowed and took a mouthful of water. 'Excuse me...'

'Alina...' He smiled. 'Everything embarrasses you. Even when you are being kind, you have to excuse yourself for not...'

'I know.' She took another mouthful of scone, just so that she wouldn't jump in and ask for more information, simply to give herself a small pause, because surely it was too personal to discuss, except Demyan had brought it up. And when her mouth was empty, the need to ask was still there.

'How bad was she?' she asked.

Her question wasn't a knee-jerk reaction and Demyan was grateful for that.

Demyan lay back and closed his eyes for a moment and tried to keep it in, but being at the farm, losing Roman, that speech last night...he couldn't.

Not today.

'If I told anyone how bad she was I knew they would take her away,' Demyan said. 'So I tried to keep her world safe.'

'How?'

'You don't want to know.'

'I do.'

'Lie with me, then,' Demyan said, not because he wanted her beside him but because he just didn't want to see her reaction when he spoke.

He told her, not all but enough to reveal the madness, the impossibility of his world—spitting three times, how you must not speak of a hopeful future, how he had left a school book once and returned to get it. 'She was screaming and dragged me to the mirror. Everything was bad omens, everything was going to ensure we went to hell. The rituals for her drinking…' He shook his head at the hopelessness of truly conveying it. 'There was so much madness.'

'So, how did you go—' Alina wondered whether she should even ask '—raising Roman? Was it hard, given all you'd been through?' Alina asked.

'It was actually easy. I had a very good rule of thumb, I did the opposite to my mother. If Roman was scared of the dark, instead of joining his fear I turned on the light and read a story. If Roman cried, I cuddled him… If he walked on the cracks, I walked on them too… If he spills salt I just brush it off.'

'Now you can just throw it over your shoulder,' Alina said, but tears in her eyes marked the solemnity of the conversation. 'How old were you when she died?'

'Thirteen.'

'Your father?'

'I don't know who he was.'

'At all?'

'He was poor,' Demyan said. 'Well, given how we lived, I assume that my mother didn't charge much.'

He knew then why he was telling her this.

Be appalled, Alina, Demyan thought.

Gather your things now and we'll head back to the car. He half hoped for it, for she was innocent and he was far from that.

Instead, Alina sat up and took another drink of water.

He watched her tongue lick over her lips and it was not a seductive move. Still, he felt it in his groin.

'It sounds as if she was terribly ill.'

'She was weak,' Demyan said. 'She chose drink…' Then he paused and looked at Alina, who said it again.

'She sounds as if she was ill.' Alina thought about what he had said about his mother not charging much. 'Is that why nothing shocks you?' she asked, and he watched as her cheeks turned to fire.

'What do you mean?'

'Well…everything shocks me. Maybe I was too sheltered. I mean, there was just Mum and I and then school was only girls…'

'We're taking about sex, yes?' Demyan checked unnecessarily. He loved it that even her throat was red and then he thought of her breasts and whether or not it was convenient. Demyan was turned on, just at the thought of her shy, and then not.

'Yes.'

They were talking about sex.

Alina lay back down.

'I don't think men…' She faltered.

'Go on.'

'Fancy me.'

'Wrong.'

'Or if they do, then they don't want to be seen with me.'

'Alina, it was work.'

'Even so, you didn't want to…'

'Wrong,' Demyan said again. 'I very much wanted to but you would have thought it…' He circled his hand and she didn't jump in. 'A date.'

'No.'

'Yes,' Demyan said. 'You would have thought it a first date and then been upset when there wasn't a second.'

'How many second dates have you had?'

'Survival rates are shocking,' Demyan freely admitted. 'If I were a hospital I'd be closed and audited.' How could his appalling reputation make her giggle? 'You will find that nice man one day, you just need confidence, experience…'

'Ah, but you can't get that without confidence and experience, it's like trying to get a job.'

'You've worked for me now,' Demyan said, and their faces turned to one another, their eyes met and held. She felt her stomach fold over on itself as she stared into unblinking eyes. 'You will have no problem getting any job you want now.'

'Are we still talking about sex?'

'Perhaps.' Demyan thought about it for a long moment. So badly he wanted to escape his own thoughts but Alina deserved more than the rather straightforward exchange that sex usually was for him. 'Just so long as you don't go falling for me.'

He was so direct, which meant Alina could be as well. 'Too late.' It was surprisingly easy to be honest lying next to the sexiest man she had ever met and she admitted a little truth. 'Kissing you took care of that.'

'Don't be so honest,' Demyan said.

'I never usually am,' Alina admitted. 'But you don't have to worry, I'm not going to fall in love, you're really not my type.'

'Am I not pale and interesting enough?'

'Too interesting,' Alina said. 'Though I do think I've got a crush on you.'

'A crush is okay,' Demyan said. 'I have a crush on you.'

'Really…' She smiled and looked over at him.

'Anyway, we can't—my jacket is in the car'

'I'm sure there are other things we can do.' Alina

smiled again. *'Anyway—'* she repeated his word '—I'm on the Pill.'

'First,' Demyan said, 'you never give that answer if there are no condoms to hand. Second…' He hesitated, he didn't really do *other* things, well, certainly not the ones she was alluding to. 'You want a man who makes love, a man who…' He just stared at her trusting eyes. 'All we are talking about is sex.'

'I get it,' Alina said. 'PA with benefits.'

This time he didn't smile because despite her brave words Alina didn't understand that he didn't do tenderness and he certainly didn't do intimacy, which was what Alina's eyes craved.

'A sex lesson,' Alina offered. She was unbelievably turned on, she could feel the moisture in her panties and could barely drag in the sultry air because it was so thick with arousal.

'No sex,' Demyan said, safe because his jacket was in the car. But he could show her a thing or three, he thought as his mouth moved in to kiss her. 'Just a lovely come.'

His tongue tasted of cherries, or was that hers? Alina thought, then she stopped thinking and just focused on the lovely feeling of his hand playing with her nipples.

Demyan had seen a lot of breasts but had never felt nipples as large as Alina's and his eyes were hungry as he removed her top.

'What *have* you done?' Demyan asked. 'How far have you gone before?'

'This far,' she said as his hand crept up her skirt. 'But not that far,' she admitted as his fingers prised their way into her panties.

'You're serious?' He smiled on her mouth.

She couldn't answer. Alina had never felt anything

more wonderful in her life, the press and the slide of his fingers over and over as his mouth worked hers. She should feel awkward perhaps, except there was no space in her mind for that. Surely it should take longer, surely she wasn't about to come.

'Demyan…'

His fingers didn't relent, but his palm was on her clitoris as his fingers slipped into her tight space and stretched.

It hurt and it was delicious and if she'd been a man it would all have been over, because she was twitching to his palm, clamping her thighs to his hand, and Demyan felt a small surge of triumph as so readily she came.

'Lick them clean…' he said, as he slowly removed his fingers and offered them to her mouth, and their tongues met as he did the same. One taste and for Demyan there was the rare need for his head to lower, for he wanted to taste her, but Alina was first in with requests.

'I want to see you too…' She could hardly breathe and Demyan felt the brush of a clumsy hand to his groin. He'd never done the fumbles and things. Demyan's first sexual experience had been with an older woman who'd shown him exactly what to do.

What was he doing in a field? Demyan thought as, instead of going straight to his zipper, she undid his shirt.

He just liked being here, hearing the birds and the sounds of nature as something terribly natural occurred; she could never have guessed that playing like this wasn't natural for him.

Demyan, Alina decided, had the most beautiful skin she had ever seen. Her fingers traced his chest and then down to his stomach as she tried to gauge the oils she'd use if ever she painted him. Linen White, perhaps, she briefly thought, but then her mind moved to other things as he lifted his hips. She slid his belted pants down, and saw the small wet patch spreading on his black hipsters, which she was going to pull down but he halted her.

'Take it out.' He liked her nervous eagerness, liked the soft fingers that traced his length and the hand that freed his balls as tentatively as if she were lifting eggs out of a nest, and then he pushed his hipsters down.

Alina had never felt or seen anything quite so lovely. Warm, straining and strong, he rose to her touch and her fingers trailed along the thick vein and then closed loosely around him.

Virgin hands too, Demyan thought as she stroked him so lightly. He took his hand and closed it around hers till she caught his rhythm then he released it so she held him solo but she kept losing her stroke. She saw him grit his teeth and she bit down on her lip and concentrated some more.

'Like that?' Alina checked as a low sound came from Demyan that was somewhere between a cuss and a moan. He swelled further to her palm and dripped to her fingers.

'Oh.' Alina had no need to ask if that was better, and he watched as greed lit her eyes and he almost came as she licked her lips.

'Can I taste?'

'Later,' Demyan said. Right now he wouldn't even make it to her lips let alone her throat, which was how Demyan usually preferred it.

He took her hand and halted it. 'I'll show you how to have a good orgasm if the loser isn't carrying condoms.' He gave a wry smile. 'The loser being me.'

He pulled her hips so she was over him.

Demyan loathed a woman on top. Control was the name of the game but he was still in charge here, which made it doable.

'Oh…' Alina said, as she felt him hard yet soft against her thighs, then she felt Demyan sliding the head of his cock against her panties over and over and even 'Oh' was too hard a word to find. Her hips were starting to move on their own, pressing down on the warm head as it butted at her soaked panties. 'Demyan…' She choked out his name.

'It's okay.' He wanted to press pause, to leave her right where she was, dash to the car, grab his jacket, put on a condom and part her panties.

'Demyan…' She kept saying his name. If he stopped she would die, if he carried on Alina didn't know what would happen. Her face felt hot but nowhere near as hot as it felt down below. She put her hand down, felt the wetness of his length and the cold wet silk of her panties. 'Is that me…?'

'Both…' He was as breathless as she.

She loved the sight of him concentrating, and, as she leant forward, she loved the sight of her own breasts near his face. His open mouth could not catch the fruit of her nipple and she deprived him of a taste as she moved to her own pleasure.

He felt her twitch and Alina felt her throat tighten at the urge to press down, to be filled. Demyan was pulling her hard onto him, digging his hands into her bottom and grinding her on him till Alina tipped fully forward and felt her hot sweaty face in his neck. She let out a low scream and Demyan held on for one reason and one reason only as she pulsed around his length.

He *had* to have her.

Demyan rolled them so she was on her back and took her tongue and suckled, then kissed her hot, tense face till she was calming, and then he told her how it would be.

'I'm going to be your first.'

Weakly she nodded. Demyan knelt beside her, and reached for a bottle and fed her a drink of water, as if she were some marathon runner grabbing sustenance while still running the race, which she was, because he was already pulling her panties down her thighs.

'As nature intended,' Demyan said.

'Maybe I should shave?'

'I shave you tonight, if you like,' Demyan said, except he rapidly reminded himself there wasn't going to be a tonight, it was just this afternoon.

'I'm working.'

She gave him an out but Demyan didn't like that answer. 'We'll see.'

What was he saying?

He didn't know and he didn't care and Alina wasn't exactly focusing on words. The lovely weight of Demyan was over her, his thigh nudging her legs apart.

'How much will it hurt?'

'How the hell would I know?'

She didn't have time to ponder his words. Alina assumed it was a facetious quip.

It wasn't.

Demyan had never bedded a less than knowing woman and had never made love unsheathed.

Sex, Demyan amended.

Make love, her heart decided as softly he kissed her mouth.

She felt his fingers again, heard them because she was soaked, and then she felt the soft batter of his rigid cock as Demyan knocked three delicious times, stretching her a little further with each one, before letting himself in.

It was the most delicious pain and Alina's hips rose as he seared inside. It was a pain that hurt less than the knowledge this could be both their first and last time.

She moaned into his mouth as the pain did not abate, and he moved deeper. Demyan could only admire her stoicism because he felt the tear and the brief jolt of shock run through her body at his invasion, then he did what he'd fought not to, he lost himself to the sensations as he inched further in.

'You'll get used to it soon.'

'I don't want to get used to it,' Alina whimpered, for could the feel of Demyan inside ever lose its wonder? How could the rhythm she was trying to match ever become a familiar race?

'You will,' Demyan said, moving in but not fully, telling himself this was no different, that he was taking his time not so he could relish the warm vice that gripped him, or the soft, yielding body beneath him—he was just trying to ensure her pleasure.

Except her pleasure was already here.

Alina first thought she had a cramp at the very tops of her thighs. As they tightened, she attempted to move, to escape, to relax, to stretch…she did not know. She felt her ankles crossing behind his, felt her hips stretch to the sky and then the ache of deep orgasm but with Demyan's mouth at her throat.

Then, as her body should be sated, as her pulse should steady from its peak, it shot up again as she heard a sound as if from behind her, yet her back was pressed to the ground. It was Demyan's passion that chased her as she felt him unleash above her, the rapid thrusts that pelted her virgin flesh were deliciously overwhelming. The mouth by her ear was delivering encumbered, illegible words that swirled her into his vortex and then released her to free-fall as his hot release procured in Alina a dense, almost reluctant orgasm. Or perhaps it was just a forbidden one, because it ended with his name, yet somehow she held onto three words that were clearly best left unsaid.

Three words that didn't make sense, Alina thought as she folded up the blanket and did her best not to meet his eyes.

How could you love someone who this time last week you didn't even know?

How could you love someone who was so clearly bad?

Demyan too was just a touch awkward driving home, he was used to a rather more seamless post-coital experience.

Namely a shower and occasionally a morning coffee.

Not picking up picnic baskets and shaking blankets and pulling grass out of hair.

Or attempting conversation on the way home afterwards.

He knew they had gone too far, or rather that he had and somehow he now had to pull back. Just as he had shrugged his aunt's arm from his shoulders on the day of his mother's burial, he tried to shrug Alina off now. As much as he might want to give in, Demyan would not.

As a familiar skyline came into sight Demyan scanned it, as he always did, for his home.

'Won't you miss this view?' Alina asked.

'No.' Demyan shook his head. 'A view is a view.'

'Will you come back at all? I mean…' Alina wasn't asking about them, she simply couldn't imagine just walking away. She still drove past what had once been her mother's farm at times; she still missed it every day. 'Won't you miss it?'

'I have never been back to Russia,' Demyan said, 'and I do not miss it at all.'

They pulled up at her apartment and he deliberately

ignored the slight sag to her shoulders when he didn't try to kiss her.

'Demyan…' She turned to him instead of getting out of the car.

'No,' Demyan interrupted, and reminded her it had been but a sex lesson and he continued it, even the difficult part afterwards. 'You just ignore that he's barely talking and you get out of the car with a wave…'

Nothing would be easier than resuming, but it would be both foolish and cruel to do so, Demyan decided.

He would not be getting closer to Alina.

In fact, he would prefer her gone.

CHAPTER EIGHT

DEMYAN WAS AT his sulking best the next day and pretty much ignored her. By Friday afternoon Alina was, at first, grateful to escape to the penthouse to ensure that every detail was right for the royal visit.

'I should be back around two or three,' Alina said as she collected her bag from beside her desk.

'Don't worry about coming back,' Demyan said, 'given that you have to be there for the inspection tomorrow.'

'I still have to let the casino know about tomorrow night and there's—'

'I can manage my social life, Alina,' Demyan said. 'I'll see you Monday.'

And therein lay the problem.

It was what happened between now and Monday that dictated their future.

Yes, it fazed her.

No, she hadn't seen it all before.

And to read about Demyan's wild weekend in the Sunday papers, to walk in on a working day to the aftermath of a decadent time was not something her heart could return from.

'Demyan—'

'I'm busy.'

It should be nice to take her mind off things, except

nothing could take her mind off him and the afternoon they had shared. She wasn't foolish enough to think it could last for ever, she just didn't understand how it had died before they had even reached the car. Alina simply didn't understand how you could move from being so close one minute to complete distance the next.

Did she regret sleeping with him?

Never.

She simply didn't understand.

Alina stared at her painting hanging on his wall and then stepped back, wondering if her work really belonged in a multimillion-dollar penthouse.

'Wow!' Libby said as she walked in.

'Too much?'

'No, that's much better.' Libby said. 'They're coming through at nine, so if we get here at seven, I'll tee up the florist and the domestic to give it a final once-over. Please let me get someone in to tidy that bedroom.'

'No.' Alina shook her head.

'They're *royalty!*' Libby persisted as they headed up to the garden terrace, but her voice trailed off as they got there.

It looked spectacular. The pool was as blue as the sky, it truly was an oasis in the skyline, it felt as if you were floating on a very low cloud.

How could he bear to leave?

She just stared up and closed her eyes and felt the warm sun and breeze on her skin and she truly didn't know if she was respecting Demyan's superstitions or secretly hoping that a guitar and a few wrappers *would* put off prospective clients, because if it sold tomorrow, it was over. Demyan wouldn't be staying to oversee the selling of the farm, that was loose change to him.

As was she.

'Alina?'

She turned around to Libby's voice.

'Is everything okay?'

'Of course.'

It wasn't, though.

As she and Libby wandered through the penthouse for the final time before inspection tomorrow, Alina found herself alone in the master bedroom, staring at her work on his wall and lost in its beauty.

It had nothing to do with ego. Alina could scarcely believe at times that the work she produced came from her.

Her gift made her believe in magic.

And even though she had nothing with which to compare, magic had happened beneath the willow tree, she was sure.

Alina locked up the penthouse and, instead of heading for home as instructed by Demyan, headed back to the hotel.

He barely acknowledged her when she arrived back.

'Demyan, I was…'

He didn't let her finish. 'I thought I said you were to go straight home.' Only then did he look up. 'I could have been entertaining.'

'About that,' Alina said, but again he broke in.

'I don't need you for anything.' Demyan said. He knew himself well enough to know he was lying. He had never needed escape more than he needed it now, but he would not inflict himself on Alina. Nadia had texted again to remind him how things stood. This time next week Roman would be on a plane, this time tomorrow his home may well have been sold, and he needed Alina tonight but would do whatever it took to resist.

'I'll call you tomorrow after the inspection.'

'Get Libby to call me.'

She could almost hear the slam of each door as he blocked contact.

'Go,' Demyan said. 'Don't worry, you'll be paid till five.'

It was Alina and not Demyan who nearly swore but she held it in. 'Demyan, can we talk—?'

'No,' he said. 'Why do women always want to talk, when really there is nothing to discuss?'

'I get that but the other day…' She swallowed and then forced herself to say it. 'If you do plan on entertaining this weekend, well, know that if you do, there will be no repeats of the other day. I—'

'I have no intention of repeating it,' Demyan interrupted. 'Go find yourself a nice boy to make love with,' he said, his skin crawling at the thought but better that than let her into his darkness. 'One who will whisper sweet nothings and take his time…'

'What if that's not what I want?'

'Alina…' He was having great trouble keeping his breathing even. 'You don't seem to understand that I was nice because it was your first time.' He watched her cheeks turn to fire but Alina stood her ground.

'So you didn't enjoy it? It was all for my benefit?'

'Actually, yes.'

'Gosh, Demyan, I never knew you were *so* into charity.' She gave him a wide eyed, incredulous smile that wasn't returned. 'Well, thanks for the donation. I didn't realise all the suffering you had to go through…' Her smile turned to a frown. 'What do you mean by "nice"?'

'You don't want to know.'

'Try me,' Alina said. 'Maybe I want what you want.'

'Then stop talking and get on your knees.' Demyan said.

He watched as her lips pressed together and saw the tears glitter in her eyes but they were angry ones.

'It really is that straightforward to me,' Demyan said. 'It is you who makes things complicated.'

'I don't believe you...'

'Still talking, Alina?' His hand reached for hers, guiding it to his zipper, but she pulled it away. 'You should be on your knees by now.'

'Screw you.' She turned for the door. 'Because it won't be the other way round.'

She wouldn't be back on Monday. Demyan knew that and he groaned in relief when she walked out.

He went for his phone and punched in Roman's number, fighting to stay calm as he was sent straight to voice mail again.

'Roman.' Demyan was sick of hearing his son's voicemail message. 'I am not sure why we're not talking but I am here if you change your mind. Call me any time.' He closed his eyes. 'Please.'

It was, Demyan knew, time to call in the big guns.

'Mikael.' Demyan spoke to another voice mail. 'Call me.'

He sat, fingers drumming, drinking cognac, waiting for the bastard to call. Demyan and Mikael went way back but, despite that, Demyan had navigated his divorce without calling on his friend. He did not need to be told his rights with his son, or how little he could get away with paying.

'What took you so long?' Mikael called Demyan straight back. He had heard the word on the streets and had long been expecting Demyan to ring. Mikael had arguably fewer scruples than Demyan and was known for going for the jugular.

'Can we meet?

They met in a bar, but the Thank-God-It's-Friday

crowd was gathering and Demyan asked to use the empty restaurant upstairs.

'What does Roman want to do?' Mikael asked, when Demyan told him that the rumours were true and Nadia and Roman would soon be moving to Russia.

'I don't know what he wants.' Demyan said. 'We are not talking and I don't know why.'

'He's fourteen,' Mikael pointed out, 'that's a good enough reason perhaps?'

'No.' Demyan shook his head. His relationship with his son had always been good till now. 'It is since Nadia announced she was marrying and decided to move back to Russia.'

'So why are you letting her?' Mikael asked the question that everyone wanted to. 'Why are you not fighting her?'

'She says Roman might not be mine.'

'Do you want to find out?'

Demyan shook his head.

'Then tell me from the beginning,' Mikael said.

'You don't need to know all that.'

'You want my advice?' Mikael checked, and Demyan gave a reluctant nod. 'Did you use protection?'

'Always,' Demyan said, then flinched a bit as he remembered what had happened with Alina. 'Always, back then.'

'But?'

'Perhaps I did not use it wisely,' Demyan admitted. He could barely remember that night with Nadia but there had been a torn condom and he might have gone in for a brief second before resheathing, he really han't been able to remember details afterwards.

'Now she says...'

'I don't care about now,' Mikael said. 'I want to know about then.'

Demyan did not want to think about then, about how then he had still thought in Russian, how his head had ached from a day speaking in English. How Nadia may well have used that weakness. 'It was nice to speak in Russian, easy to end up in bed. By morning I was over her.' Demyan took a belt of his drink. 'A few weeks later she told me she was pregnant. I was a lot younger back then, I knew I had slept with her. I dealt with the consequence and we married.'

'You never doubted her?'

'No.'

'Two years later, you divorced. Why?'

'Because.'

It was impossibly hard for him to dissect it, to sit with Mikael when deep down he knew that there was nothing he could do to help.

He was desperate, that was all.

'We divorced because the man with a promising future wasn't delivering quickly enough.'

'And…'

Demyan paused. Mikael was only the second person to ask him such direct questions. Alina was the other but he simply wasn't ready to answer, even to himself.

'Soon after the divorce I started to do well,' Demyan said. 'Then I started to do very well and Nadia wanted us to get back together. She still does. I have always said no.'

'Always?' Mikael checked. 'I need the truth.'

'Always,' Demyan said. 'When I am done with someone I don't change my mind.'

'How much do you pay her?'

'What is right,' Demyan said. 'I don't want to go into figures.'

But Mikael did. 'Nadia has never worked a day in her life, she comes from the streets like us, so where is she getting the money to live as she does?'

'Me,' Demyan admitted. 'I had a single mother, I did not want my son…' He faltered. 'She has raised him well.'

'On your money.'

'Of course.'

'So, prior to her bombshell, what was supposed to happen when Demyan turns eighteen?' Mikael asked, and Demyan shrugged. He didn't like this conversation, didn't like where it was leading. He didn't like a mind that was as dark as his voicing his thoughts.

'The money to Nadia will stop then.'

'It *has* stopped now?' Mikael checked, and Demyan swallowed. The afternoon sun streaming through the windows was too hot, the noises from the bar below were too loud, though but not loud enough to drown Mikael's words. 'You're not *still* paying her?' Mikael had the guts to smile into the black face of Demyan. 'She tells you that Roman is not your son and you still write a cheque.'

Mikael had a solution, or the start of one. 'I will have her served on Monday, letting her know that if she takes him to Russia, then every cent you have paid her over the years you are claiming back, every dollar you spent raising her bastard…'

Mikael didn't get to finish. Demyan's fist was in his face, and Mikael just laughed and hit him back.

'Fool, Zukov, she treats you like a fool and you let her.'

It wasn't pretty. Demyan went ballistic. Mikael didn't mind in the least; it had been way too long since he'd had a good fight.

'Like the old days, but with tasers,' Mikael said, as the police did what they had to do to subdue Demyan. No, Mikael told them. He would not be giving a statement or laying charges and neither would the restaurant, given the cheque Mikael was writing.

As the police took a cuffed Demyan away to cool his heels in the cells, Mikael had the last word. 'Don't waste my time, Demyan, until you're really ready to fight her. *Then* you can call me.'

Alina was just getting in from work when her phone rang.

'Senior Constable Edmunds, from Kings Cross Police…'

Alina rolled her eyes when she heard that Demyan had been in a fight. 'You have a set of keys apparently. He's lost his.'

Alina was tempted to tell the senior constable that Demyan was no longer her problem but hearing the music coming from her house she told herself that was the reason she was heading back into the city.

She surely couldn't want him after the awful things he had said?

Surely.

'You don't look pleased to see me,' Demyan said, as he took his belt and tie from a bored officer, pocketed them and then signed his release forms, as Alina sat there, legs crossed, tapping her foot in the air. Did he have to look so amazing? There was a bruise to his eye and his knuckles were grazed and his suit was torn, and even from this distance she could feel his unpredictable mood.

She glanced around the police station as she stood. 'It's not exactly my idea of a fun night.'

'I show you the world.' Demyan shrugged as they headed out to her car.

'I rather prefer my world.'

'Ah,' Demyan corrected, as they drove from the station, 'but from what you say, you don't.'

Alina indicated left to head for the hotel. She knew he was referring to their earlier conversation at the hotel but she refused to jump at the bait.

'Home,' Demyan said, and reached over and flicked the indicator to turn right as Alina gripped the wheel. 'I am sorry to call you out this late…'

'No, you're not.' Alina turned briefly and looked at him.

She was right, he wasn't sorry at all, for were she not here, God knew where he might be now. Demyan's world was out of control, just tipped off its axis, and he wanted it back in place.

He was on the edge of emotion and it was a place he avoided at all costs, a place he chose not to visit. Yet tonight he could not escape.

'I had a fight with—'

'I don't care,' Alina broke in, telling herself that she just wanted him out of her car, just wanted her boss delivered home, and after the inspection tomorrow she would have no dealings with him ever again, but Demyan continued speaking.

'I had a fight with Mikael,' Demyan said. 'My lawyer.'

'Oh, very wise,' Alina snapped, as Demyan answered his phone.

'Mikael…' He chatted for a few minutes and Alina simply didn't understand. Yes, they were speaking in Russian, but what she didn't understand was that the conversation sounded amicable. 'He has called to see how I am.'

Alina shrugged.

'What I said back at the hotel—'

'Was crude.'

'But necessary,' Demyan said. 'You deserve some-one less…' He paused. Out of the corner of her eye she could see his hand circling but it wasn't shyness now that kept her from jumping in, there was no one word to describe him.

'You might not understand but I was trying to look out for you then. I don't do tender, I don't—'

'You did,' Alina choked. 'When we were at the farm…'

His head felt as if it was splitting, his body ached from the taser, his heart was screaming for his son, and there was nothing left but his billions.

They approached the building and she turned off the engine and removed his keys.

'Come up,' Demyan said, because he could not stand to be in there yet he could not bear not to be.

'No, thank you'

'You have to come up, I can't remember the security number.'

'Liar.'

'Come up,' Demyan said again.

'Why?' Alina challenged. 'I might want to do some-thing unspeakable, like talk, I might want—' She never got to finish. Demyan's voice broke in and told her the truth.

'You know why.'

She did, it was there at her base and there was this ripple of delicious fear as she stepped out of the car that she was about to see the real Demyan, the other real De-myan that she so badly wanted to know.

'Demyan—'

'I have no wish to speak.'

'Then why did you call me?'

He chose not to answer that. Instead, he gestured with his hand as the elevator door opened. 'After you.'

'I'm quite sure the doorman would have let you in,' she said to his closed expression, watching as a muscle pounded in his bruised cheek, but she refused to reduce what was between them to nothing. 'Or you could just have gone back to the hotel. If it was meaningless, name-less sex you wanted, why did you bother to call me?'

'You know why.'

Alina blinked. She *didn't* know why and then it dawned that possibly Demyan was telling her that it wasn't meaningless, nameless sex that he wanted tonight. She actually heard the whistle of air in her nostrils as she breathed in a strange mix of anger and arousal—the scent came from her.

Alina stepped out and Demyan walked behind her; she could feel his eyes on her as she opened the door.

This time as she punched in his number her hands were shaking but for a different reason. Demyan was at her neck, his erection pushing in her skirted bottom, his hand at her breast.

'Demyan, I don't think—'

'Don't think, then. And don't talk.'

His mouth was hot at her neck, his hand pulling up her T-shirt and then removing it as he rubbed against her. He was animal. Alina had never felt anything like the pas-sion that blazed from behind her; it both unnerved her and excited her. Deftly he removed her bra so her breasts sprang free and his fingers bit into the soft flesh.

She wanted to stop, to shower, to slow things down.

'I've been working, Demyan…'

'Don't argue with me now…'

It wasn't his command but his fingers sliding into her skirt that made her stop, and the pressure on her clito-ris that made her throb. She tried to turn around but he held her firm, just enough so she couldn't. Or rather, as his hand released her, she didn't, and when Demyan lowered himself to his knees Alina went *with* him onto hers,

If she hadn't been so turned on, Alina might have been scared, except he had flicked the switch and there was nothing she would deny him.

Alina heard the slide of his zipper and felt the coolness of air as he ruched up her skirt and pulled down her panties.

'Demyan...' Alina was shaking, shocked to her own core at the knowledge he could do anything. His hand roamed the curve of her bottom, and she closed her eyes, bracing herself, just handing herself over to the scariest, most beautiful man who in that moment she had little choice but to trust. And at the base of her soul she did. Her eyes opened, as did her mouth as he seared inside her. Alina's jaw gritted as he met her cervix but there was a strange giddy relief in her head and she started to come.

Demyan was thrusting and Alina's head was on her forearms yet her neck arched back as deeper he ground, pulling her hips back to his in tune, meeting his urgent want.

One orgasm ran into another, the second so strong that Alina almost crawled on her knees to be away from him, but he held her tight and she went with it, sobbing and choking back the tears as her buttocks and thighs clamped the small of her back to an arch and he swelled further inside her.

'Alina...' He lost his head for a moment, and said things he did not mean as he came, that he loved her, that he was crazy about her, that she'd saved him, but they were all said in Russian, Demyan consoled himself as he slid out of her.

'Come on...' He picked her up, as if she weighed nothing, and Alina didn't argue, her legs were incapable of walking. She had no idea she was the first woman he had brought up these stairs and to his bed and she lay there watching him shrug off his clothes. He caught her eyes.

'I've a feeling we're not in Kansas any more,' Alina said, and Demyan gave a thin smile and climbed into bed.

'You make a very nice Dorothy,' Demyan said, and attempted a very brief kiss but it turned into just a little bit more.

'Sleep,' Demyan said, pulling back.

Amazingly she did.

He did too but only for a couple of hours. He woke and looked at Alina asleep next to him. His ribs hurt but he moved to his side and looked at her.

Had she not picked him up he'd be back in the cells by now, Demyan knew.

He wanted to kiss her awake, to make very slow love, but he didn't do that sort of stuff and, anyway, she looked too peaceful to wake.

Instead, he got up and wrapped a towel around restless hips and roamed the penthouse.

Demyan didn't even bother to put on the lights.

He knew this place like the back of his hand.

It was the only place apart from the farm where he had ever felt settled. Each hotel was the same but different; here had really been a home.

Demyan headed to Roman's bedroom and hesitated before opening the door.

He'd told Alina he didn't want to know if she did have it tidied and cleaned. Demyan knew that the superstitions were just that, old tales, but he had been raised on them, brought up to believe that danger beckoned, had had his mother's mad rambling repeated over and over so much so that he could hear it now.

His brain in business was logical yet he almost folded

over in relief when he opened his son's bedroom door and it was just as he had left it.

Alina had understood how much the small ritual meant. Even Nadia, who was Russian, had laughed when Demyan had asked she keep the room the same when Roman had had a fever and been taken to hospital.

Nadia.

The name made him feel ill.

Demyan sat on the bed and picked up his son's guitar. He glanced at a picture of Nadia and heard her voice again.

'My period was already late when I slept with you.'

He could still hear her saying the words, telling him that the sexy young Russian, with a serious future ahead of him, was a more palatable father than the married professor she had been seeing the past few months.

Roman was his, Demyan had been sure of it, not once had he thought otherwise.

He looked at the photos of his son.

The image of Nadia.

Yet he was deep like he himself was. He liked words; he liked to sit in his room and did not desire company at times.

Nature or nurture?

Demyan put down the guitar very carefully and left his son's room as he had found it then went back to bed, but he did not sleep.

Alina's phone alarm went off at six, the room in darkness. She looked at his back, could see from the set of his shoulders that Demyan was awake. As her eyes grew accustomed she could make out the bruises. Her hand moved to his shoulders and she felt the despair and the tension in them. 'Demyan…' She wanted more, wanted to know more, and she wanted to give now rather than be taken.

Demyan closed his eyes as her hands worked his shoulders, rolling onto his stomach and almost giving in to the bliss of her bottom on the small of his back as her hands soothed him and then her mouth on his neck. He turned over and looked up at her.

'I make coffee…'

'Demyan…' She didn't understand him, could feel him hard, nudging against her, and it had been okay when he had been showing her, teaching her, but it apparently wasn't okay now. So badly she wanted to make love to him yet, like Demyan, she refused to beg.

'Two sugars,' Alina said, and rolled off.

He kissed her sulking mouth. 'You remind me of a much nicer version of me,' Demyan said, and got up.

'I'm not sure that's a compliment.'

'Oh, it is.' He pulled on black jeans. 'I'd better get dressed, I don't want to scare the florist…'

As Alina lay there, trying to fathom the unfathomable, Demyan added two shots of cream to his and two sugars to hers and was glad that they would have visitors this morning because it would be rather too easy to head back to bed and start over again.

He had far too many feelings for Alina and he would prefer not to examine them.

'Demyan…' Alina had other ideas. She really wanted to talk and it would be far easier out of bed. She was at the top of the stairs and wrapped in a towel, Demyan at the bottom holding the coffee, when the door opened and both were met by angry, accusing eyes and teenage rage.

'Is this the reason you don't fight for me?'

'Roman,' Demyan shouted as the coffee landed on the

floor, but Roman wasn't waiting to listen to his father. Hurling abuse, he turned and ran.

'Some *souka* shows up and you...'

'Roman!' Demyan roared. Alina fled back to the bedroom and sat on the bed, her head in her hands, as the door slammed, only to be opened by Demyan and not even closed as he sped out after his son.

The alarm went off just to confuse things and Alina sped down and was punching in the numbers, wearing only a towel, as Libby arrived. She gave a very subtle eyebrow rise at Alina's appearance and then glanced down at Alina's waitressing uniform on the floor.

For Alina, to have her private life, her very new, very private sex life, exposed like that was excruciating.

She dressed in yesterday's clothes but the hooks on her bra had been flattened by Demyan's less than patient attempts to get it off.

She doubted he kept safety pins!

And it wasn't just the eye roll from Libby but the florist coming in as she tried to make the bed.

Alina took herself out of the way as best she could, standing in the terrace garden as the royal couple and their entourage made their way through. There was no sign of Demyan.

She'd expected no less.

'They didn't give away much.' Libby caught up with her after they had gone. 'I'll let you know as soon as I hear anything.'

'Thanks.'

'Alina...' Libby could see her discomfort and tried to put her at ease. 'It's forgotten, it never happened...'

It never should have, Alina decided.

Demyan returned just as Alina was leaving. She didn't care if he'd lost his keys, or how he might get in.

She was beyond livid.

'Have you any idea how embarrassing that was?'

'Alina, my son turned up…'

She really was in no mood to discuss his domestic life. 'Well, he clearly gets his foul mouth from his father. How dare he speak to me like that?'

She was beyond reason. It was all horrible and wretched and really no one's fault but she was in no mood to see that. 'I'm going.'

'Where?'

'Where do you think? Home,' Alina said. 'Oh, but that's right, you wouldn't know what that was—after all, you're getting rid of yours.'

She stood there, waiting for him to match her anger, to tell her not to leave, to offer to drive her, hell, call a taxi even, but Demyan was clearly more than used to an angry lover's silent demands and he was also terribly used to ignoring them.

'You're not staying for coffee, then?'

She could have slapped him. She wanted to slap him but there was simply no point.

'Go ahead,' Demyan said, glancing at her clenched fists, but instead of slapping him Alina let out a sob and turned and ran.

You signed up for this, Alina reminded herself as she shivered on the bus ride home, remembering the teary women leaving his room.

Why had she expected anything different from him? He was leaving, could it be any clearer? She was the one helping to sell his home. How foolish to think, for even a second, that it might be different for her.

Demyan was terribly used to slamming doors—really, did women close them any other way after a night in his bed?

What he wasn't used to was that gnawing of disquiet. Neither, when he should be thinking of the conversation he had just had with Roman, was he used to lying on a bed, hands behind his head, staring up at the ceiling and looking at the world from her vantage point.

'I don't need this,' Demyan said out loud, because he really did not need feelings right now.

He had no intention of going after her, she was far better away from him, and, Demyan thought, noticing for the first time the picture she'd had hung, what the hell had she done to his wall?

Talk about how to put potential buyers off! Alina had said the room needed a few feminine touches but there was a blown-up nipple hanging on the wall.

Or was it an ovary?

Demyan was no art snob and barely gave paintings a glance; if he did, he was far too sullen to comment. But this *thing* on his wall was actually rather fascinating. So much so that Demyan peeled himself off the bed and went in for a closer look.

How could a flower be sexy? But it was. Lush and ripe, it just throbbed on the wall. The artist had somehow put the human into biology. It reminded him of that dress she had worn. And then he glanced down and saw the signature.

Alina.

Bright and beautiful, Demyan thought, but, like the pregnancy that had carried her, complicated.

CHAPTER NINE

IT WAS A busy night and terribly hard to smile and be polite and discuss the specials on the menu when your head was locked in a war zone called Demyan.

She ached.

Not just her heart but also her body.

Alina was swollen and sore from their lovemaking, she was tender all over, and now, if she didn't want to upset Pierre, she had to paint on that smile.

'Alina!' Pierre snapped. 'Quickly to table four. He's back.' Then she turned and her heart almost stopped.

There sat Demyan, a lazy smile on his face.

'How can I help you?'

'Do you really want me to answer that here?' He said and then saw the shimmer of tears in her eyes.

'You were right,' Alina admitted. 'I'm not up to this.'

'Meaning?'

'In a couple of weeks you'll be gone.'

'What an amazing couple of weeks we could have,' Demyan said. 'I want to get to know you, Alina.' Even if he had no soul to offer, he could leave her with the gift of herself. 'I want to know who you're hiding yourself from.'

'I'm not hiding.'

'What's the bravest thing you have ever done?' Demyan asked, and he watched as she struggled to answer.

'I'll tell you—it was when you came back with me last night. You took a risk, a chance...'

'It seems terribly foolish now.'

'You regret it?'

'No.'

'Then take another risk,' he said. 'Come out with me tonight.'

'I've got to work.'

'After work,' Demyan said, but she shook her head. 'Be with me during the time I have left in Australia.' Demyan made a scissors sign with his fingers. 'It's time to snip that safety net.'

'If I wanted psychological advice you're the last person I'd go to,' she said, but it just made him smile.

'What's stopping you, Alina? What's stopping you from having fun and living as you want to?'

'Roll up, roll up, Demyan's in town, but then you'll be gone and I'll be left with the muddy field.'

'You've got boots in your car.'

She closed her eyes.

'You can do this, Alina.'

Could she, though? 'How?'

'Just be yourself.'

'I am.'

'Not quite,' he said, because he'd seen her pictures, he knew there was so very much more. 'But you'll get there. For now, what's on the menu?'

'A promiscuous Russian and a naïve farm girl.'

'Sounds very tempting.'

'It is.' She took out her pad. 'What do you want to eat?'

'You choose,' Demyan said. 'Surprise me.'

'I doubt that I can.'

'Oh, I'm sure that you could.' He confused her, he tested her, he challenged her. 'Off you go.'

'What does God want?' Pierre asked, when Alina had left Demyan's table. He blinked at Alina's response but just a little. Demyan could have whatever he liked.

Which was the problem.

Pierre would never guess they were lovers, no one could know the sex that was burning in the room as Glynn brought him his drink.

'One Nothing Left to Lose.' Glynn smiled and as Demyan caught her eye, Alina smiled too as he called her over. 'What's in it?'

'I haven't a clue,' Alina said. 'The name seemed appropriate.'

'It tastes sensational.' He made her feel weak as he rolled the beverage on his tongue and then swallowed. 'I taste Yellow Chartreuse,' Demyan said. 'It is a liqueur made from a secret recipe by monks...' He offered her the glass to taste but Alina shook her head.

She was working.

She could feel his eyes on her as she worked and her body thrummed with awareness, all her senses heightened. She was petrified to go to the loo, quite sure that in the smouldering mood he was in Demyan would have no qualms about following her in. She was on a delicious edge, so much so she almost shot out of her skin when the bell went and his food was ready.

Demyan looked down.

'We're skipping straight to dessert,' Alina said. 'To the best bit. It's the nicest thing on the menu.'

'You like crème brûlée?'

'Yes, but that's lavender crème brûlée. It's delicious, one taste and you swear you could eat it for ever, but it's very rich...'

'A treat.'

'An *occasional* treat,' Alina said, trying to tell herself

that this was not love, jut a delicious dalliance she would soon tire of. 'Enjoy.' She went to go but he stopped her.

'Bring me another.'

All night he teased her, all night they played till Alina's skin was burning, and she was grateful to end the shift without dropping a pile of plates. She could hardly breathe as she stepped out of the restaurant and to his mouth.

'I want you.' His tongue had the last traces of her favourite thing in the world and his erection was almost painful on her bursting bladder.

'I need to go to the loo...'

'I *needed* you to go to the loo...' They were filthy kissing between laughing. 'Be bad, Alina.'

'I can't be.'

'You're in my world now.'

'When do I sleep?'

'Monday, eight a.m.' Demyan said, between hot, urgent kisses as he pressed into and tried to breathe his bad into her. 'I tuck you into bed in my hotel and I pay you to sleep. Or is that inappropriate?'

'No,' Alina breathed, but as his fingers moved up her skirt her hand halted him. '*That's* inappropriate.'

'Funny girl.' He looked at her. 'What do you want to do?'

'I don't know.' She was on a high she had never been on. He was back and it was like nothing she had known. That she had him, even if for a little while, was the most delicious treat and she would not waste their time with shyness.

She had perhaps a few days, maybe a couple of weeks with the most beautiful billionaire in the world, and she had no intention of looking at prices.

'I want to go to the casino opening.'

'What else?' Demyan said. 'Tell me, don't hold back, what do you think a night in my world is like?'

'I don't know…' Alina begged, 'Sex on the beach…'

'You can do better than that.'

She was holding back because otherwise she'd be being taken in the street yet he pulled back a little from her and God help Demyan because the brown eyes that met his were just so clear and non-calculating. She could have asked for her pick from any jewellery shop and it wouldn't have been about money, just escape, just… His mind searched for the word and it had nothing to do with language, because the word had never existed for Demyan till now.

Fun.

He partied, he did whatever pleased him.

It had never been as simple as fun.

'What does Alina love to do when she's not being a PA or waitressing?' He smiled a slow lazy smile as he looked at her, waiting for her to reveal a bit more of her truth, but still Alina resisted, and for now Demyan chose not to push.

'Come on, then…' He kissed the tip of her nose before taking her hand. 'We go to the casino.'

'I didn't RSVP.'

'Good, then we make a better entrance.'

'Can I go and have a shower?'

'No point,' Demyan said. 'You'll still smell of sex.'

Sydney was pulsing, the crowds building as the rich and famous gathered to celebrate the opening of the luxurious complex.

They drove past the red carpet where lights were flashing as security tried to hold the gathering crowd back, and Alina blinked as they drew up at a side door and she realised that again it was her turn to get out.

'You can be such a bastard without even trying,' Alina hissed.

'You want to go on the red carpet in your waitressing outfit?'

'Of course not.'

'Then go and choose something to wear.' The door was being opened by two burly security guards.

'Demyan, I have no idea what to get.'

'You had no trouble choosing the other night,' Demyan said, opening his wallet and handing her a card. 'Go, get your hair done or whatever. I wait for you here.'

'Demyan, the other night...' He waited, waited for her to tell him that it had been a dress that had been born from her own hands, but instead she shook her head. 'It's not just about money...'

'It has *nothing* to do with money, it is what you think of you,' Demyan said, ignoring her frown as she tried to make out his words. 'I'll wait here.'

Because the new casino was strictly by invitation for its opening night it was heaving with beautiful people. It was also laden with shops that Alina would never think of going into had she not had Demyan waiting outside.

First she found a bathroom and had a quick wash as she gave herself a small pep talk. To hell with being nervous Alina decided as she headed out to the boutiques and walked into the one that beckoned the most.

'I need a dress for tonight.'

'Did you have anything in particular in mind?' An assistant gave a very nice smile. 'This is just in...' She held up what to Alina looked like a huge black cape.

'I like colour,' Alina said, her eyes homing in on an incredibly slinky number, the Monet of dresses—it was lilacs and greens and the prettiest of whites. It came with its own built-in underwear that tamed her breasts but did not contain them, and had small poppers in a crotch that Alina struggled to do up.

Yes, she loved colours, Alina thought as the experts dealt with her face and hair, and soon she was staring in the mirror at silver-lilac eyelids and a mouth painted pink that might look sweet were it not so wanton.

And Alina liked glossy curls.

And naming beautiful shoes.

Alina tried to decide between I-Lost-It-To-Demyan shoes, which were willow green and had six-inch heels, and Take-Me-From-Behind shoes, which consisted of heels, a single purple strap and not much else.

'Both,' Alina said, as she stared down at her pretty feet. 'I'll take both.'

He would not recognise her, Alina thought as she stepped out of the shadows and into his car.

He did.

It was the woman who had opened the door to him that night of the ball, a woman who smelt of summer and anticipation, a woman whose river ran deep for she kept her secrets hidden.

'*Tiy viy-gli-dish' kra-see-va.*' He said what he had said the evening she had opened the door in that amazing dress.

'You have a thing about my nipples, Demyan.'

'I do,' he freely admitted, but he told her the truth now. 'It actually means you look beautiful. You did then and you do now.'

With Demyan she felt it.

It was giddying, stepping out to the cameras and to the shouts and cheers because Zukov was there, but who was this woman on his arm?

'Your friends will get a surprise...' Demyan said, as they danced through to the small hours, for they would be all over the papers tomorrow.

'My friends won't even recognise me,' Alina said, and it came with a bit of a jolt that Demyan had. That this version of her, the one who felt more like herself than she ever had, was one that neither her friends or family had met.

They headed to the gaming rooms and, yes, Alina turned heads.

What was it? she mused.

Because she'd have felt like a Christmas decoration had she worn this dress just a week ago. Now, though, she was on fire.

'I'm going to win.' She knew that she was as he kissed the dice in her palm and his tongue met her skin.

She was.

Alina simply knew it.

Tonight a win was inevitable.

'No!' Alina screamed, when the gods didn't oblige.

'Again,' Demyan said, urging her on.

'Ow!' she screamed, when still the stars did not align.

'Again,' he urged. People were starting to gather and she turned to him, to his kiss, to her winnings.

'I can't wait for the beach...' Demyan moaned to her mouth, for he had organised a helicopter while she'd shopped.

'I can't either.'

'I mean, I can't *wait*.'

'Me too.'

He kissed her all the way up in the elevator, his tongue almost savage, but Alina's was too. He nearly had her in the hall. She was vaguely aware of a butler rapidly disappearing as they fell through an open door.

Those tiny poppers that had been so hard to do up were her undoing now for Demyan was inside before the door even closed. Frantic, urgent sex where she could barely even lift her legs, such was the force of the man pinning her down.

'God, Alina...'

It was new-shoes-worthy sex, it was amazing sex. There was nothing she could complain about for she was shouting his name too and coming as rapidly as Demyan...

It was the aftermath that confused.

She lay there, staring up at the ceiling with Demyan on top of and inside her, and then turned her head slightly and looked around.

They were in a very luxurious suite, but a different one. Though it was similar to the one she had become used to.

It took a moment to register that he must have booked them into the casino hotel.

What man kept two presidential suites on the go?

It took another unsettling moment for Alina to realise that she hadn't even known where she was.

CHAPTER TEN

ALINA WOKE TO the sound of Demyan talking on the phone. He was speaking mainly in English but his sentences were peppered with Russian words and when he turned off the phone and sat on the edge of the bed, Alina had already worked out he'd been speaking with his son.

'That was Roman,' Demyan said.

'That's nice.'

'He wants to meet. Probably for another row but better that than…' He gave a tight shrug. 'I don't know how long I'll be.'

'It's fine.' Alina said. 'It's good that he called.'

Demyan gave a small nod and she found she was holding her breath, waiting for him to say something, to let her a little bit into that part of his life.

'You'll miss him…' Alina attempted.

Demyan didn't answer.

'Can I ask…?' She didn't even finish her sentence as his eyes told her that she couldn't enquire about his son, about the reasons he wasn't fighting to keep him. 'You tell me to be myself.' Alina looked at him. 'Well, *she* has questions.'

'Alina…' Demyan actually wanted to tell her but how could he? It was the most dangerous secret and Demyan was doing everything he knew how to contain it.

'Yes?' She stared back at him. 'You said my name. Alina. Generally it's followed by something.'

'Not this time.' Demyan stood and went to kiss her but she moved her head.

Last night had been the best night of her life yet this morning all that she felt was cheap.

Alina tried to go back to sleep but couldn't.

She ordered breakfast but could only pick at it.

Was she supposed to just lie here and wait? He wouldn't come back, Alina was sure of it, and if he did—for what?

Certainly not conversation.

It was then that Libby called her with the news that an offer had been made on the penthouse, one so good that Alina didn't have the authority to decline.

'I'll put it to Demyan,' she said, and hung up the phone.

It was over.

She climbed out of bed and picked up her dress.

Of course he'd torn it.

Well, she wouldn't be walking out with her breast exposed. She'd damn well ring down for some clothing to be sent and charge it to his bottomless pit.

Alina headed to the shower and stood under the stream of water and started sobbing.

She just stood there sobbing, not because of last night but because of tomorrow and the next day and then the next one.

After Demyan.

He let himself in and sat on the bed and heard her sobbing. Demyan put his head in his hands. Her tears did not distress him. After all Roman had just said, Alina's sobs matched his mood.

Every shudder from her lips felt like his head, every

angry moan felt as if it was coming from him, but he remained silent.

Under any other circumstance Alina would be mortified to have been caught so bitterly crying but as she stepped into the bedroom, though at first she was startled to see him sitting on the bed, as he looked up, his grief was so evident that there was no room for embarrassment.

Fear had her running to him. For a second she actually thought his son must have died.

'You are the only person I can discuss this with…' His voice was hoarse. It was a shocking admission for him; he even hesitated now from revealing it.

He never asked another for advice.

Yet he wasn't his mother—where his son was concerned, Demyan was not too proud to ask for help. Instead, he was strong enough to change and so he forced himself to continue.

'You are the only person I feel can speak with. For the first time, I honestly don't know what to do.'

Oh.

Life had been one constant surprise since she'd met Demyan but perhaps this was the biggest of them all.

'Roman might not be mine.'

Alina was wet from the shower, on his knee, trying to scramble, to shoot down fears, to give an instant solution. 'He is.'

'He might not be.'

'There's DNA.'

'And then what?' He tipped her from his knee and stood, almost appalled by his own revelation. Yet the words had finally been said and he turned to look at Alina, who was pulling on a dressing gown, trying to wrap her head around what he had told her.

'Does Roman know?' Alina asked.

'No. This morning he asked why I am letting him go to Russia, why I don't put up a fight. He thinks I don't love him…'

'Then you have to let him know that you do.'

'If only it were that simple.'

'Demyan, you're involved, it could never be that simple,' Alina said, and he knew then he had chosen wisely. He even managed a pale smile before explaining some more. 'For a long time Nadia has wanted me to get back with her.'

Alina tried to ignore the squeeze of fear to her heart as this was not about her.

'When I refused to even discuss things she said she was marrying Vladimir and taking Roman to Russia to live. Of course I told her that would never happen. I don't want him in Russia, his home is here…' Demyan closed his eyes as dark memories swirled, there was nothing nice he could remember about his homeland.

'I knew she was trying to make me jealous, I said that I would have a stop put on Roman's passport and that I would contact Mikael. I said that I wanted my son to finish his schooling here, that when he was eighteen then he could make a decision but till then…' Grey eyes were black now when they turned to Alina. 'It was then that she told me there was a very good chance that Roman was not my son. To challenge her legally I would have to find out if Roman is mine.'

'He already is.'

Her simple statement halted him and Alina spoke on.

'That's never going to change. You were there when he was born, you told me you were, all the memories you've made, all those times you've shared can't be erased by some test.'

'Not for me,' Demyan said. 'But what if it changes things for Roman? I can't stand to lose him.'

'But you are already,' Alina said. 'In his eyes, you're doing nothing and so this way you are.'

Demyan could not stand it, there was no solution that he could see and his mind always sought a solution. He always controlled situations but now, when it mattered the most, he was shackled by the ghosts in the closet. Perhaps he hadn't chosen so wisely, for Alina was suggesting that he let those ghosts of the past out.

'I think you have to speak with him,' Alina said. 'I think he has to know the truth.'

'You think, do you?' Demyan was at his derisive best but she refused to be deterred.

'Do you want my thoughts or not?'

He did.

'Not here,' Demyan said. He was sick of hotels, they all looked the same, they all felt the same.

He wanted home.

CHAPTER ELEVEN

DEMYAN HAD NEVER taken advice on parenting.

He did it at gut level.

It was the reason he had never consulted lawyers during his divorce. Amazingly, neither had Nadia—she had known she was getting an incredibly good deal.

He had never paid much attention to the magazine articles written about him either, for Demyan had known, despite their suggestions otherwise, that he would be home for Christmas and all the things that mattered.

That he listened to Alina was more of a compliment than she could possibly know.

Even though he refuted the words that came from her lips, the fact that a discussion was taking place was a miracle in itself.

They sent out for food, they drank wine, they argued and paced rooms and split hairs about the most precious detail.

His son.

And she found out that when Demyan loved, he loved for ever.

'He leaves tomorrow, I can't just walk up and say to him that he might not even be mine.'

'I get that!' Alina said. 'I get that it's going to hurt him…' They'd come from Roman's shrine of a bedroom and were upstairs in the master bedroom, Demyan staring out of the window, trying to wrestle his mind from resistance, and then he flinched as Alina told him her shame.

He flinched for her, although he already knew.

'It was my dad that I was trying to contact when I was on your computer. I sent him a friend request,' Alina said. 'He should have jumped to respond to me, he should have spent the last twenty-one years trying to be a part, even a small part of my life. You're blocking Roman.'

'I'm not.'

'That's how he sees it. To him, you simply don't care enough to fight.'

Perhaps, Demyan conceded, but only in his mind.

He needed to think, or rather not think for a while and let the thought simmer. The very idea that he might tell Roman the truth had felt like annihilation. Now, though…

'Can you talk to Nadia?' Alina asked.

'We are so past talking.' he said. 'She's counting on it, though. She will have something up her sleeve, you can be sure of it.'

Alina had nothing up her sleeve—in fact, it was Demyan's last card that she brought to the table now. 'There's been an offer on the penthouse, a good one. After you left this morning, Libby rang.'

'I assume, given the buyers, it's not subject to finance?'

It was a very thin joke and they chose not to smile. It was a mere matter of signatures now.

'I have no choice but to let him go. Maybe some time in the future we can talk…'

Alina took a deep breath. 'Will you make Russia your base rather than Sydney?'

Demyan didn't answer. He could feel the clock ticking down on Alina and him and there was so much he still had to find out, so much she still held back.

He felt her hands on his shoulders and on instinct he shrugged her off and then relented, but only, she realised, because he had a question.

'Why were you crying?' He felt her hands pause. 'Alina?' He wanted now to get to them, he wanted to know more about the woman who might just be capable of changing his mind.

'I think we both know.'

'Say it.'

'Because we'll be over soon,' she said simply.

Say it isn't necessarily so, her eyes begged, give me one shred of hope. But he kissed her instead, a deep, deep kiss that tasted urgent, a hungry kiss that stripped them in moments, and as he pushed her to the bed, Demyan chose not to think about anything that might possibly hurt.

Alina defied him. Slow were the kisses that met his mouth, far from urgent the body beneath him, for she wanted more than the urgent sex that displaced her and so she fought to explore every inch of him. Instead of succumbing, she etched him to memory with her mouth.

'Alina…' Her lips brushed over his eyes and it was the most intimate kiss Demyan had ever allowed, and they were unfamiliar waters he was sailing on as he rolled to his back and she kissed down his cheek and chin and he tried to claim her mouth but she resisted.

She kissed his eyes again and he could not stand the bliss, could not bear to succumb, to give in to her mouth, so he chose words to halt her.

'I know about your art…' Her mouth paused, but she would not let him distract her. 'That you don't have the guts to display it.'

She would not give in to his taunts, she would not stop, she *would* explore every inch of him in her own time. Her tears fell on his lips and he tasted her salty warning and stayed silent as she worked her way down.

Alina shaded the dark of his nipples with feather-light strokes and added a dash of desire and cardinal red to her palette and resumed, sucking on the flat nub, hearing his ragged breathing, his hand trying to guide her head down.

No. Still, she did not relent.

It was time for his stomach and she painted seashell white with a dash of linen as she deep-kissed his pale skin. Demyan's hands pushed at her head but she denied him. Instead, she shaded in the snake of hairs, and each slow brush of her lips had his fists clench tighter.

'Alina!'

She ignored his protest, though, and down her mouth slid till she painted his intimate length, holding it, exploring it at her leisure, denying him as he tried to thrust it in her mouth and just soft-kissing the swollen head.

His hand pushed her down. 'I show you how,' he said, yet she refused to be one of Demyan's perpetual puppets.

'I don't need to be shown,' Alina said. 'I've never tasted you there before and I want to take my time...' He was the best thing she had ever tasted and she relished him with her mouth. Lost to his intimate scent, she curled her tongue around his length but Demyan did not want her to take time, he did not want the mouth that moved slowly back up his stomach and left him aching. Demyan did not want more colour added to his chest.

'Why can't you relax?' Alina asked.

'Because the second I do, the ground cracks, the sky...'

'No.' She kissed his mouth but he turned his head away.

'I'd prefer your mouth somewhere else.'

'Tough,' Alina said, because no longer did he offend her. 'I want to kiss.'

'I want to come.'

'Why the rush?' she said, though her mouth did move back down to meet his aching length.

He wanted to give in, to just lie there and let her; he wanted, he wanted so much so that even as his hand pushed her head down he almost regretted it, for her kisses were so teasing and sweet.

She was swirling his head with her tongue, soft, gentle sucks, rising instead of lowering when he thrust his hips. It was driving him insane. If she would just obey his hands he would bury himself in her and force her to a more rapid conclusion, yet she would not move.

Demyan went to her hair, tried to guide her with his hand.

He *had* to come.

'If you push my head down one more time,' Alina said, 'I'll tie your hands to the bed…' She faltered. She hadn't meant it like that but as their eyes met for a long moment, perhaps, Alina realised, she had.

'Other way round,' Demyan said.

'Not *always*.' She smiled and got back to teasing his length but as she gave him head she was struggling to keep hers, to be strong, to be herself, to not submit to a man who refused to submit. Alina adored the taste of him, loved the feel of him almost writhing as he tried to stay still. There was a building tension in him and it was flaring also in her. Slowly she relished him, took him just a little deeper, teased him some more, but as she pulled back and blew on him, then, just as she was about to give in, to take him deeper, to succumb to his will, Demyan got there first.

He rolled her, a wedge of muscle hauled her up the bed and onto her back. A shocked, excited laugh came from Alina, as he held her wrists over her head.

She was laughing as he parted her thighs, ruing that her game had gone on just a little too long, but next time…

He felt her writhing, fighting the constraint, burning beneath him but laughing too, and then he felt her start to come.

'Always,' Demyan said, as he pulsed inside the malleable mystery woman beneath him and, hell, who could resist exploring that side of her?

Not he.

'Nearly always.' His mouth smothered hers and he brought her back to the world with a kiss he had so often refused as his last two words played repeated in his head. Demyan was, for the first time, factoring a known woman into his future, bringing her into his world. 'Maybe there is something to stay for,' he said.

'Don't.' Alina shook her head. 'Don't say things that later you might not mean.'

'I might mean it, though.'

'Now,' Alina pointed out, 'and then you might not.'

'What are you scared of?'

'The truth?' Alina asked, and he nodded. 'I'm scared of spending the rest of my life looking out for a man and wondering if he'd even recognise me if we saw each other again.' She was trying not to cry. 'I still look for my dad. That first day we met, when you were having lunch, I was eating my sandwich…'

'Hotdog,' Demyan corrected.

'You were watching me?'

'I couldn't take my eyes off you,' he said. 'I still can't.'

That post-orgasm high was fading, but Demyan's feelings were still there. He was actually relieved by the alert on the intercom because he was precariously close to telling her he loved her again, but in English this time.

'Roman?' Demyan called out, because only Roman could let himself in like that and he could hear him punching in the code. He pulled some clothes on as Alina scrambled out of bed and pulled on her skirt and searched desperately for her bra as quickly as she could, hearing the footsteps on the stairs and the door opening.

'Just me, Demyan,' Nadia said, and, completely naked, she walked into the bedroom.

CHAPTER TWELVE

IT WASN'T THAT Nadia was naked that froze Alina, instead it was the look, or rather the non-look, she briefly gave her.

Dismissive, just so, so dismissive.

Without so much as a word Nadia told Alina that she didn't factor a jot in this.

'Demyan, *ya khochu*—' Nadia started.

'It isn't about what you want!' Demyan both shouted and translated. 'You will speak in English in front of Alina.'

It was perhaps the polite thing to do but Alina rather wished she'd never had to hear it.

'I want us to be together again—a family,' Nadia rasped. 'I think I've made the most terrible mistake…' She started sobbing. 'Demyan, what I said about Roman, it was a lie. I wanted to make you jealous, hell, I wanted you to react…'

'You come here to tell me you lied?' His voice was clipped but his breathing ragged. 'You show up here in my bedroom… How the hell did you get the code?'

'Roman,' Nadia said. 'Roman gave it to me because he wants us to get back together too, Demyan…' She continued, 'I don't want to take Roman from you. This way we can be together.'

It was too much for Alina, and with a sob she turned to run.

'Alina!' he called. 'Alina,' Demyan roared as she fled down the stairs.

He caught up with her in seconds.

'If we have any chance, you have to hear this…'

'I shouldn't *have* to hear this,' Alina flared. 'I shouldn't have to see this. You've been divorced for years.'

'You know the reasons why she's here, though.' Alina was the one person he had told, and his eyes demanded that she understand. 'You need to hear it firsthand.'

'Demyan, your ex-wife is naked in your bedroom…'

'This has *nothing* do with Nadia,' Demyan said, and to prove it he picked up the clothes Nadia had strewn on her ascent up the stairs.

'Get out,' he said to her. It was a voice only a fool would argue with and Nadia, Alina knew, was no fool. Her beauty mocked Alina over and over as she dressed, her confidence, her absolute assuredness that Demyan was hers taunting Alina as she walked past.

'I fly tomorrow,' Nadia said, and blew him a kiss. 'Come and say goodbye if you choose.'

Alina went upstairs and retrieved her bra and she turned from him as she put it on.

'We need to talk.'

'Oh, that's rich, coming from you,' she said.

'We need to talk,' Demyan said again.

'Then answer this—have you thought about getting back with her?' She turned and looked into eyes that looked straight into hers as his mouth lied to her.

'No.'

'I hate that you just lied.'

'I hate that you gave me no choice but to lie. If I'd said

yes you'd have run off before I'd even finished the sentence. What are you running from, Alina?'

'You!' Alina shouted. 'All this. I can't do it, I don't want to do it.'

'I tell you why you run from me. I make you be yourself. When you run from me you are running from you. Why are you dressing in a suit, trying to be a PA...?'

'Trying?'

'You're actually not very good!'

'Bastard.'

'Of course I am, but if I said that about your artwork, you'd have slapped me.'

Colour scalded her face. 'I don't want to talk about it.'

'No, you want it hidden in a wardrobe, or hung on a wall in someone's home when you should be showing it to the world.'

'Actually, you're wrong. I've just booked a stall at the market.'

'Market...' Alina could not possibly have chosen a filthier word for Demyan. His mind flicked back thirty years to a life that every day, every hour, every minute he did his best to forget. To hunger and filth and the tricks his mother had been reduced to just to make the rent. 'You won't be working in a market. Your work should be in a gallery. I can—'

'You'll buy me a career, will you?' She didn't want to hear it, he turned everything on to its head. 'You'll give me everything and then leave me with...' She was almost gagging, trying to hold back tears, because he was offering more and then he would leave.

'I'm not your father, Alina.'

'Don't even go there.' Her face twisted in suppressed rage. 'Don't make promises you can't keep.'

'Talk to me...' Demyan urged. 'Alina, please...' He

was locked in urgency; the whole of Sydney glittered behind her shoulders, and it was a view that almost soothed him. 'Alina, I am trying to make the biggest decision—'

'Get on your knees, Demyan.' She hurled his crude words back at him, assumed he was talking about Nadia, and right now she would prefer torrid sex than confrontation, but he gave just a wry smile because on his knees he wanted to be…

…in proposal.

'Talk,' Demyan said. 'Row if we must but I'm not the only one who has stuff to sort out, Alina.'

'Then sort it,' she said. 'But, please, do it well away from me. She shook her head. He was just way, way too much for her. 'I want my life back, Demyan.'

'Alina…'

'I mean it, Demyan. I want my life back. I want to go home.'

'No, you don't,' He was sure of it. 'Come on, Dorothy, click those heels…'

'I don't want your black brick road, Demyan.' She didn't, she wanted safe, she wanted this done, she wanted this over, so she could commence her healing now rather than later.

He would be gone, Alina knew.

'You're sure about that?'

'Very.'

'I don't nag.'

'Beg,' Alina corrected.

'I don't do that either.'

He wanted to call her back but stood there. For a small moment he had glimpsed a different world and he truly did not know if he was capable of it, this home filled with laughter and fat babies and telling Roman at the airport tomorrow that he always had a home here, in Sydney, with him and Alina…

He looked out of the windows at a view that had for a second again soothed him, but the magic was gone now.

Fool to think it could be different.

Alina was right: she was better away from him.

CHAPTER THIRTEEN

HE NEITHER NAGGED nor begged.

Alina wanted him to, though, but it was all over by ten past nine on Monday.

'Well done!' Elizabeth said. 'Demyan called and said how well you'd done and he's forwarded a very glowing reference.' Alina closed her eyes. 'You'll go places now, Alina.'

Places that she didn't want to go, yet in his black way, with his glowing reference behind her, Demyan was pushing her towards her vision of safe, rather than towards being the woman she really wanted to be.

'I've got a very nice position in the CBD,' Elizabeth went on. 'It's for three months and it's a full-time position.'

'I'll get back to you.' Alina said, when usually she'd have jumped at the chance of three months' full time work.

She should have stood her ground with Demyan, Alina knew that. She knew she should have had a little more faith in them.

But, simply, she didn't.

When the doorbell rang her heart leapt in foolish hope. She peered out of the window and saw the silver of Demyan's car.

She almost wept in relief as she opened the door but instead of Demyan it was Boris with a leather-bound folder.

'Mr Zukov has asked for the return of any keys and also the elevator pass.'

'Of course.' She got them from her bag and signed them over.

'He'll organise the leased paintings to be returned once the property sale has been confirmed.'

'Leased?'

He handed her a contract.

When it was over with Demyan it was completely over.

'That's not necessary.'

Alina took the paper, and stared at it for a moment.

'Could you pass on a message?' Alina asked.

'Of course.'

'Remind him that the seemingly worst PA in living memory had his home sold in just over a week.'

She closed the door but less than twelve hours after she'd denied him she was calling his phone—she didn't need Boris to pass on her messages, she would tell him herself.

Of course Demyan had blocked her number and it hurt, it hurt like hell, it hurt way more than it had when her father had done the same.

He had severed every avenue.

Over the next couple of weeks Alina became almost as superstitious as Demyan.

If she turned off her phone and didn't check it for an hour, with no cheating, he'd call her.

He didn't.

If she was cheerful and happy at the restaurant, maybe she'd turn around and find him watching her.

It never happened.

She turned down another job offer from Elizabeth but, the golden PA she was now, Elizabeth persisted.

'Two months' work in London?' Elizabeth offered. 'It's an amazing package, actually…' And Alina listened as she heard she'd be flown there and her rent would be paid, because with Demyan's reference behind her there was nothing she could not achieve.

'No, thank you.'

'We have had a call though that you might be able to deal with. Apparently he left a jacket at a property in the Blue Mountains.' Alina frowned. As far as she could remember, his jacket had been in the car. 'Normally you'd tell people to post it, but given it's Demyan I'm sure he'd expect the golden gloves. It will add up to four hours' work for you. If you want to drive over and get it I can ask where to forward it.'

'I could drop it into the hotel.' Alina's voice was a husk. Finally there was an almost legitimate reason to see him.

'Oh, no,' Elizabeth said. 'He's back in Russia.'

Stupid to expect or hope for anything else really.

No goodbye, no kiss, nothing.

It wasn't as if she hadn't known how it would end from the start, Alina told herself. After all, her first introduction to Demyan had been that teary trio leaving.

Why should she be different?

Why should she think that what they'd had had been any more?

Because it *had* been more, she tried to tell herself, but wavered, because in Demyan's arms she felt beautiful and sexy and wanton, but out of them she was well above her ideal weight and as bumbling and shy as ever before.

'Oh…' Elizabeth continued. 'And the real estate agent

called. The painting in the bedroom—the prospective buyer wants to know the artist…'

Alina felt her heart squeeze and then stopped herself. It was Demyan, just trying to boost her confidence, trying to buy her the career that she wanted.

'I can't remember,' she answered.

It was a beautiful drive, even if her heart was heavy. She remembered each bend in the road from the last time she'd been here.

And it hurt to remember,

Hurt even more to drive into the farm where she had spent that glorious afternoon with Demyan, to look over to the creek and see the green trails of the willow dipping into the water, to remember the balmy shade and the cool green light in the place he had taken her and made her his lover.

'Alina.' Ross looked a lot younger and a whole lot more relaxed than the last time she had seen him. 'Thank you so much for coming. We tried ringing but we couldn't get through.' He led her into the house. 'It's a very expensive jacket.'

He probably had five hundred of them, Alina thought, but she just gave them a smile and thanked them.

'Would you like to stay for lunch?' Mary offered.

'No, thank you.' Alina forced that smile. If she stayed she'd end up breaking down.

'Do stay,' Mary insisted. 'We want to pick your brains. Are you in touch with Demyan?'

'Not really.'

'Only we're trying to work out how to thank him.' Mary shook her head. 'How do you thank someone for that, though?'

'For…?' Alina frowned.

'Giving us the farm!'

Alina blinked. They clearly thought she already knew as Mary continued. 'I got the shock of my life when I opened the door and there he was with all the paperwork handing over the farm to us—I thought it must be a mistake, but…' Mary started crying and Ross continued.

'Never for a moment did I expect him to do that. I remember him as a teenager, a right sullen young man he was. "There's trouble," I said to Mary, but how wrong I was. He's saved us twice.'

Alina did stay for lunch. Ross and Mary wanted to reminisce and Alina so badly wanted to hear, she wanted to know everything about Demyan. She wanted to gather every little piece of information that she could and just take it out piece by piece and, no, she was nowhere near over him.

Soon she would be over him, Alina said to herself, but she knew she was lying.

'He used to steal food when he first lived here,' Mary reminisced. 'Katia couldn't understand where it all went then she found it stashed in his bedroom.' Mary smiled. 'I guess none of us have ever been truly hungry before.'

'Were they close?' Alina asked. 'Demyan and his aunt?'

'Eventually,' Mary said. 'She was ever so proud of him. I remember his wedding…' Her voice trailed off. 'It was hard, Katia had just been diagnosed.'

They spoke for hours and at the end of it Alina felt drained, just not quite drained enough to leave him behind for ever.

'I was wondering…' She felt awkward, standing at their door, holding onto his jacket and making such a request, but Alina knew it was her only chance. 'Could I take a walk?'

'Of course you can.' Mary smiled. 'You must miss the country, it stays in your blood.'

'I'll say goodbye here,' Alina said. 'It's been lovely, talking.'

She walked down to the river and slipped under the tree. Yes, she could take photos and try to capture it in her art, but photos weren't the same. She could feel it, she would remember it for ever, lying here, being made love to by him.

Alina buried her head in the silk lining of his jacket and wept till there were no tears left, wept as she never had before and hoped she never would again, because she felt so sick after.

It was just hard and a shock, such a shock that he'd sold the house.

The silk of his jacket was cool on her hot, swollen cheeks as Alina got to the gulping stage.

She parted the branches and looked over to the farmhouse where a young Demyan had once lived. The same house he'd hoped to raise his child in but Nadia had had other ideas.

Alina didn't.

She'd dared to dream, she'd been foolish enough to let her mind wander, but this was where the dream ended.

She'd imagined them here in this house with their baby and now that too had been taken away from her.

'We'll find somewhere,' Alina said to her late period and very sore breasts.

She was still too scared to confirm it.

She was, though.

She knew it.

She'd had her cry.

Alina threw the jacket on the back seat of her car.

Now she just had to get on with things.

CHAPTER FOURTEEN

THE WORLD WASN'T KIND, Alina decided.

A kind world should surely follow certain rules.

There should only be ancient magazines in doctors' waiting rooms.

Not glossy up-to-date ones with photos of Demyan and his son, walking along, both smiling, their breath blowing white in the cold Russian winter.

She flicked the page and stared down the long lens of the paparazzi and into the ritzy restaurant where he sat, chinking glasses with Nadia and Roman.

But was he happy?

Her eyes searched his features and Alina truly didn't know.

Probably.

Demyan didn't exactly laugh easily but in that photo in the restaurant, with Nadia and Roman, he clearly was.

Would it make it easier if she thought he was acting, that he'd gone back to Nadia rather than lose his family?

'Ms Ritchie?'

Alina stood as her name was called and followed the doctor into her office.

There was so much hurt that all Alina felt was numb.

'I'm pregnant.'

Of course, the doctor wouldn't take her word for it

and Alina handed over the mandatory urine sample and gave dates and things as they waited for the predictor to change.

'You certainly are!' The doctor hesitated and glanced at her lethargic and rather pale patient. 'Are congratulations in order?'

'They will be one day.' Alina said. 'It's just a bit tough right now. I was on the Pill but…' She shrugged. No, she hadn't set out to trap him, just a little white pill had been so easy to forget when you were preparing to step onto a red carpet and falling in love when you had promised yourself you wouldn't. All that should have been important and sensible had disappeared, thanks to the most dizzying, complicated man.

'The baby's father…' the doctor probed.

'Is back with his ex-wife.'

Oh, it was a sorry tale and no doubt to the doctor it was a familiar one.

'He still has responsibilities.'

Alina gave a tired shake of her head.

'Have you told him?'

'He's moved overseas. He was only visiting Australia for a couple of weeks,' Alina said.

Foolish girl.

And, yes, one day she'd have to tell her child who its father was, but the future felt a terribly long way off when you were having trouble getting your keys out of your handbag.

There was one good thing about having a broken heart, though, one good thing about insomnia and a heart that was so bruised Alina was aware of each painful beat.

Her artwork.

She ran, to herself.

Alina moved out from Cathy's and rented a tiny apartment but it was *her* tiny apartment. It was bliss to have her work left out, to have things untouched and no parties or noise as she lost herself in her work.

In her paintings she found herself day after day, night after night.

Buds of lilac that tasted of his kisses, and sunflowers and yellow roses and willows that dipped into water, but that wasn't right...

Yes, she had stuff to sort out too. Demyan had been right because she painted holly and not with Christmas in mind. It meant—*am I forgotten?*

It was for her father, not that he'd ever see it, and the prickles cut deep as Alina shaded them in.

Then her heart returned to Demyan.

She painted and painted—Yellow Chartreuse liqueur that had rolled on his tongue, but in Alina's style. She explored the flowers in the secret recipe that had graced his lips, the violets and saffron, the sharpness of citrus that had been the ingredients when there had been Nothing Left to Lose.

She had everything to lose now.

Alina cried as she painted their story, but they were healthy tears, good tears as he escaped through her fingers and, like the tiny life inside her, Alina grew.

So lost in her work was Alina she nearly didn't hear her phone but whoever it was they were persistent.

'Alina, it's Elizabeth.' Alina stared at the piece she was working on as Elizabeth spoke on. 'I have a very exciting offer just in. Two months in Dubai and there's a substantial bonus for you at the end.' Alina swallowed as she considered it.

The money was amazing and her pregnancy wasn't showing yet. She could return in eight weeks with security, except she had a stall booked to display her work. The easiest thing would be to say yes, yet she could almost see Demyan's black smile as she took the easy option.

'Alina?'

'Elizabeth, it sounds amazing but I'm going to have to say no. I've got other work organised.'

She almost called Elizabeth back. Her work at the café might last a while longer, but single motherhood and waitressing at night wasn't exactly a mix. She could get ahead now, Alina told herself, and concentrate on her artwork once the baby was here... She was so torn that she answered the phone without thinking, and then she heard a voice that had her heart racing all over again, propelling her to run, just as she should have the first night outside the restaurant.

'Alina...'

She almost folded over at the sound of his voice.

'I hope you don't mind me calling you. I just wanted to see if you were okay.'

That was a lie. Not a complete one. He needed to know that she was okay, but more than that he needed to hear her voice, a voice that had always soothed him.

Just not today.

'Why wouldn't I be okay, Demyan?' Alina's voice was sharp, bitter but better that than broken. 'Oh, that's right, sorry, I forgot, I'm supposed to be pining.'

'Alina,' he said.

'Curled up on the bed, or drowning my sorrows in wine. Sorry to disappoint you...'

'You never once have.'

She closed her eyes at the slight huskiness she heard near the end, which told her that he was hurting too.

And to make herself strong Alina picked up the magazine she'd swiped from the doctor's and stared at the images.

I hate you, Nadia.

Alina had never really hated in her life, but she looked at the supposed beauty and was filled with loathing at a woman who could use her child as a pawn.

And Alina wasn't one for double standards, which meant she wouldn't be using her own child either.

She'd tell Demyan about the baby when she was safely over him, when she could do it without breaking down.

'What do you want, Demyan?' she demanded, and when the line was silent, her bitterness spilled over like black champagne, 'How's Nadia?'

'Alina. I know how it looks—'

'You know nothing,' Alina hissed, and hung up the phone.

CHAPTER FIFTEEN

DEMYAN HEARD THE click of the phone as the lifeline that he needed today was terminated.

Perhaps it was for the better.

Some journeys were easier shared but perhaps better taken alone and Demyan was so much stronger now than then.

He hadn't even told Roman where he was today. He would bring him here to visit her grave when the time was right. Demyan had spoken at length with a priest who had agreed with Alina that his mother had been ill, desperately ill.

He stood at the soft mound of soil, already partly covered in a fall of fresh snow. He had heard no screams of protest from his mother this time as she had been lowered and Demyan's heart was at peace for she could now rest in the ground of the church. Now he could remember happier times. Now that she was here he could stand and remember not the fear but the love, and there had been love. This time when he walked away he did not need to look back.

She was resting peacefully now.

It was hard.

But not the hardest part to this day.

'Ya tebya lyublyu, syn.' As he had when Roman had

been much smaller, Demyan told his son, in Russian, that he loved him, when they met.

'*Noh?*' Roman asked.

'There is no "but",' Demyan answered in English. Roman's Russian was good but it did not quite stretch to this conversation.

The hardest conversation to have.

But it was a necessity, Demyan had decided.

Lies had come between them these past months and the truth could no longer make things worse.

'Your mother does not want me to have this conversation with you,' Demyan said, 'but I have told her that I must.'

There was the crunch of snow as they walked and the air was so cold that it burnt to breathe it but the words that came were not frozen or bitter, they came from summer and love. 'She told me something that I believe she used as a weapon against me,' Demyan said, 'but that weapon has since turned on you and I. We are barely speaking.'

'You have your…' Roman hesitated. Growing up, his father had never so much as tapped him but that morning when Roman had hurled words, once his father had caught him Demyan had shaken him till his teeth had rattled for saying such a thing. 'You have your woman to speak with.'

'Alina,' Demyan said. 'Her name is Alina but right now—' He didn't get to finish.

'And my mother's name is Nadia,' Roman interrupted, and Demyan halted at the threat in his son's voice. Yes, he had said less than pleasant things to Nadia but never when Roman had been there, Demyan was sure of it. Then his heart stopped beating for a couple of seconds, it just stilled in his chest as Roman turned to him and Demyan realised that he didn't have to tell Roman the dark truth, for it would seem his son already knew. 'Whatever she might have done in the past, my mother's name is Nadia.'

Demyan watched as Roman's dark eyes filled with tears and he was so, so proud to see them. Proud, not just of Roman, for even if incapable himself, he had raised a son who could show his emotions in the most natural of ways.

Maybe he wasn't so incapable of showing emotion for, as Roman spoke on, it was Demyan who felt moisture in his eyes.

'And my father's name, whatever happened in the past, will always be Demyan.'

It was discussed without words, it was said without saying.

Whatever some laboratory decided, Demyan was Roman's father.

'I do want to be in Russia,' Roman said as they walked further and talked more deeply. 'I want to learn about my culture, I want to learn the language better. Can you understand that?'

'Of course,' Demyan said.

He had never wanted to return but now that he had, through adult eyes he could see its beauty.

It just didn't feel like home.

'Who is this Alina?' Roman asked.

'We are not seeing each other,' Demyan said. 'She was working for me.' It was pointless to lie, he simply could not dismiss her. 'We were seeing each other for a while but it did not work.'

'Why?'

Demyan told him that it was personal. 'We will get a drink.'

They walked into a bar and sat at the counter. 'When I was younger, before my mother was so ill, we would come here some mornings. She worked at the market and I would come here and have kasha.' Roman pulled a face, the thought of porridge not appealing. 'I had it with jam,' Demyan said, and he sat there remembering days that he had never thought of before. His mother waving a spoon at his face, smiling and laughing as she cajoled a small child to eat. He remembered too the feel of her picking him up, ruffling his hair, before her illness had taken hold.

No, he had not done the opposite of his mother with Roman—the beginnings of a parenting manual had been put in place by Annika. He had known love and affection, but only now could he remember it.

As they were served their drinks at the counter Roman, as gangly teenagers often did, knocked the salt. Black eyes met his father's and though Demyan had done his best not to pass on the superstitions, he saw in Roman that slight start of fear. But Demyan smiled and took a pinch and threw it over his left shoulder.

'I do that,' Roman said, 'when you are not looking. A friend showed me that.'

Demyan smiled. 'Here, we don't throw it, but a friend showed me that too…' Except she was far more than a friend to him. 'Alina,' he corrected. 'Alina showed me that.'

Roman pushed for more information when perhaps he should not have, but he had never known his father with anyone. 'Alina is the only woman you have ever brought to our home. Were you serious?'

'No,' Demyan said, and remembered how he had smiled more than he ever had when he had been with her. 'We were rarely serious. Except when we argued, of course.'

'Not many people argue with you.'

'Not true,' Demyan said, and he thought of Mikael. They had worked these streets and knew how it was, so it was safe to fight with him. He thought of Nadia but he did not argue with her, which infuriated Nadia so. Demyan did not argue with Nadia because he did not care…

He cared about Alina so.

Loved Alina so.

So much so that when his phone rang Demyan smiled as he took the call.

'She said no to Dubai?' Demyan was still smiling when he hung up the phone. 'Go, Alina!'

There was a job, he'd ensured that with Hassan, but it warmed his heart to know she hadn't taken it, that Alina was surely following her own path. He looked at his son.

'Do you want some relationship advice from someone who has never held one down for very long?' he asked, and Roman nodded. 'Sort yourself first,' Demyan said, because how he wished he'd met Alina tomorrow or next week, yet he might never have made it to this point had it not been for her. 'Know yourself first.'

'That is what I am doing,' Roman admitted. 'I know you were not keen for me to come and live here but I want to be here, I want to know my history.' He swallowed. 'I think I want to find out…'

'It's okay,' Demyan said. 'You have every right to know.'

Roman looked at his father and they had always been close but never closer than now. 'What would it change for you if I found out?'

'Nothing,' Demyan said. 'I have been through it and over it and have grieved and I am still standing.'

'You're sorted, then.'

He was, Demyan realised.

Just a little too late.

As Roman checked his messages Demyan did the same. There was one from his online 'friend'—Alina's father. Demyan had never responded to him but he kept trying to worm his way in.

Watch your daughter soar, you bastard...

Demyan tapped it in and then deleted it. He would save his moment but he would have it, Demyan was sure.

He wasn't his mother, trapped in an illness, he could change. And he wasn't Alina's father either—he would fight to keep her in his life.

Fight to make her a part of it.

CHAPTER SIXTEEN

DEMYAN SAT in the restaurant and watched as Alina took out her notepad and took orders from a large, noisy table. Her hips were bigger, her bottom fantastic, her breasts, well… He blew out a breath and decided it was safer for now not to look there.

He looked at her very pale skin and the dark rings under her eyes and she was either pregnant or she had the heaviest period in the world.

He hoped it was the former.

Not just because he hoped she was pregnant—Alina was still a little bit shy and he had every intention of bedding her soon. He didn't want her embarrassed because she had her period.

He'd work on it, Demyan decided.

Every day, he would work on her shyness and the heart he had damaged so.

His eyes said that as she turned and saw him.

She didn't go pale, she didn't drop anything, her eyes just brimmed with tears and she shook her head.

'Table four—Zukov,' Pierre instructed.

'Can Glynn serve him?'

'He's asked for you.'

And what Demyan Zukov wanted he got.

Not this time.

No.

Her heart quite simply couldn't take it. A few weeks ago Alina would have run to him. Now there was another heart beating inside her and her child would never be used as a pawn in the Zukov game.

'You're looking very well…' Demyan said, when she stood at his table.

He couldn't know, he *must* not know.

'I've been hitting the hotdogs,' Alina said, and, yes, she could admit to mourning him, but she had to let him know she was over him now.

She had to get him out of her life.

'I start my diet on Monday.'

'Pity,' Demyan said.

'What do you want to eat?'

'I want a cocktail,' Demyan said. 'You choose which one.'

'I'll get the wine waiter.'

'I went to your apartment…'

'I don't live there any more,' Alina said as he looked through the menu.

'Tell me the dish of the day.'

'Please don't do this, Demyan.'

'I'm hungry.'

She read out the dish of the day, she was beyond games now.

'You didn't take my calls.'

'I never will.' She looked at him. 'I'm done.'

'You mean, we're done, which means I have a say in it.'

'Don't you try and correct my English,' Alina snarled. 'I'm done. What you want doesn't come into it.'

'Tell me the dish of the day again and the chef's special selection.'

'Sure.' She blew out a breath. 'Some messed-up Russian and for an extra treat we throw in his naked ex-wife.'

'You forgot the teenager.'

'Roman was never an issue.' She could not bear it. Could not stand it. Would he not just get the message and leave?

'I would like the soufflé…'

'No,' she said, because it took too long. Pierre looked around at the snap in his waitress's voice. 'Demyan, just go…'

'No.'

He was going to stay to the end of her shift, she knew it. He would eat and eat soufflé and she could not stand it.

'Fine,' Alina said, and wrote his order down and added the cocktail of her choice.

She would rather lose her job than succumb to him again.

She handed in his order and then, without a word to anyone, she took off her apron. As unrebellious as ever, she mentioned to Glynn that table seven wanted a lemon, lime and bitters.

And then she slipped out the back of the kitchen, past the bins and into the street.

And she ran.

Demyan waited.

'One Black Russian.' Glynn put his drink down and Demyan felt as if he knew her soul, for she would never choose black. Alina wanted colour and light.

He heard Pierre complain that Alina was taking too long. Saw Glynn come out from the kitchen, shaking his head, and before his soufflé was even being whipped, Demyan knew she had gone.

'Where's Alina?' Demyan demanded of Pierre.

'Alina…' Pierre hesitated. 'Glynn will take over your table,' he said, beaming. 'Is there anything I can get you in the—?'

He didn't even wait for Pierre to finish speaking. He strode into the kitchen, oblivious of the protests from the staff as Pierre frantically attempted to smooth things over.

'Where's Alina?' he demanded, heading to the women's restrooms now.

He'd lost her. Demyan felt a flare of panic. He didn't know where she lived any more, he knew her in his heart, yet logistically he knew so little.

Demyan ran through to the street, terror clutching his heart that he might have missed her, cursing himself for not telling her his truth there and then, sure he had lost her. But suddenly there she was, running.

Running from him this time, instead of running from herself.

'Alina!'

She heard his roar but she just ran faster. 'Alina!' He was easily closing on her, her head start diminishing with each of his long strides. He caught up with her and grabbed her arm and her body halted, almost defeated because with just one touch he claimed her again. 'You will listen to me.'

'No.'

He swung her around.

'You will.'

'No.' She did as she had as a child and put her hands over her ears to block out words, because she knew how dangerous they were, how easily he convinced her she was the only one. 'I don't want to hear it, Demyan, I'm not going to listen.'

'You will listen.'

'I won't!' She just kept talking, telling him over and over that she wasn't going to listen, till he put his hand over her mouth and told her that she *would* listen.

Alina bit him, dug her teeth into the softness of his palm and bit down and then bit harder. As he gave a stunned 'Ow', she released him.

She stared wide-eyed, unable to believe what she had done. She could taste him on her shocked lips and she waited for a slap, or *'souka'*, or for his true colours to show, still not understanding they had long since been revealed to her.

'Bad girl!' Demyan said, shaking his hand, which throbbed. She really had sunk her teeth in. *'Bad* girl!'

He started to laugh, as Alina stood there incredulous, not just at his reaction but that she had bitten him. He brought out every part of her—the wild, the shy, the timid, the good, the bad and the animal—and she was crying and laughing and just helpless when he pulled her back to the arms she craved.

His hands roamed over her. She could feel his warm palms over her arms, down her waist, over her bottom, over and over as if he'd missed her body for ever and ever. She wanted him to stop, wanted to tell him to get his filthy, Nadia-stained hands off her, but just one more moment...

One more.

He was kissing her face, her cheeks, her eyes, his lips wet with her tears. 'Here or bed?' he asked. 'I tell you here or bed.'

'I don't want to hear it.' There was nothing he could say. An occasional mistress, even a regular one.

She couldn't be that, yet right now how she wanted to be.

'Here or in bed,' Demyan demanded.

And who was she to deny that she wanted his words, wanted some hope of closure? She prayed for anger to return and make a sensible woman of her as she heard his appalling excuse. The thought was enough to part her face from his.

'Does your ex-wife not understand you, Demyan?'

'You understand me,' he said, 'or one day you will, but for now you understand me more than anyone.'

Okay, so he won a brief taste of her lips, but Alina tried to stop herself, pushed on his chest to lever her mouth from his for her lips just refused to obey her command to desist.

'Are you staying together for the sake of the children?' she taunted.

'Child,' Demyan corrected. 'Really he is a young man but, to answer your question, no, I would never stay for the sake of the children.' Because he was now sure she was pregnant, he wanted to make himself clear. 'I tried it once. I will not make the same mistake twice.'

'Then why?' She sobbed it, almost screamed it, so loudly that passers-by turned round. And *finally* she did not care what others thought of her, her hurt was too much to contain. 'How could you go with her? How could you not come and find me…?'

'Because this messed-up Russian had a lot to sort out before he came to you. A lot,' he reiterated, 'but I promise you, I have not slept with Nadia, not one kiss. She leaves me cold. She has left me cold from the first time I slept with her.' He grabbed her hand and crudely brought it to his crotch. 'Nadia…' he said, and smiled at her. 'Nadia… if you wait a moment it will go down.'

'Stop it,' Alina begged. 'Stop your games, your lies.'

'Never,' he said. 'This is not a game and I never lie.

Bed or here?' he said again, and she knew it was his final offer.

'Bed.'

'Tut-tut-tut,' Demyan said. As his mistress he could have made her. 'Remember the number?' he asked as they stepped into his home.

'You didn't change it!'

'I didn't change a thing.'

He hadn't told her he loved her, but as she walked into his house, Alina knew then that he did. Somewhere in the future, if she ever doubted it, if ever she forgot just how much he loved her, all she had to do was remember this.

She was everywhere, Alina realised as she wandered around.

Her wine glass was still on the table, not a thing had been tidied or changed.

It had never been nicer to come home to a messy house.

She walked upstairs and there was her hair tie on the pillow of an unmade bed and it was all just as she had left it.

'Where have you been sleeping since you came back?'

'At the hotel,' Demyan said. 'I could not bear to be here without you.'

She tasted his tenderness then. Not for the first time, but it was the first time that neither pretended this love was not real.

His mouth roamed the changes in her body, her swollen areolae and then down, ever down to intimate, engorged petals that dripped with a nectar more designed for him than any bottled scent.

She tasted herself on his lips as he spilled inside her

and she would taste him for herself one hour soon, she said, yet Alina still hadn't told him she was pregnant.

Demyan lay there and wondered whether, had he not found her, she ever would have told him.

He felt her surface from orgasm, back now beside him. It was question time.

'Did you think of going back to her?'

This time he didn't lie. 'Yes, I thought about it, if it was the only way I could keep Roman, but the more I thought about it, the more I knew I could not have another marriage for the sake of a child.' There was just a touch of colour flooding her cheeks. 'No point,' Demyan said. 'Then my mind moved to other things.' He smiled.

'Like?'

'Taking your virginity.'

'What were you doing in Russia?'

'Sorting things out.'

'With Roman?'

He didn't answer.

'With Nadia?'

'A bit.'

He heard her sharp intake of breath and he told her something he couldn't tell Mikael, something Alina might not understand.

'I never loved Nadia and I have always told myself I gave our marriage our best, that it did not last because I did not make enough money...' He turned and told her the rest of the truth. 'My aunt was sick when I married Nadia, I was as closed off as I have ever been. I owed Nadia an apology. The death of our marriage was not all about her,' Demyan said, 'but mainly I was in Russia to sort out me.'

He told her about his mother, how he had arranged to have her buried in consecrated ground, and Alina started to cry when she realised that she'd hung up on him on what must have been his blackest day.

'It was a good day,' Demyan said. 'A necessary day, putting old ghosts to rest. Afterwards I spoke with Roman.'

'Did you tell him?'

'There was no need,' Demyan said. 'He knew. He is a bit mixed up whether or not he wants a test…' He gave her a smile. 'Any more questions?'

'Dinner with Nadia?' Alina scowled.

'Because I don't care about her. I can have a drink with her on my son's birthday and perhaps in the future attend his wedding—there's no feeling there other than I want to do the best for Roman.' Demyan had questions now. 'What have you been doing?'

'Painting,' Alina admitted. 'A lot. I've got my first stall at the market…' She actually saw his cheeks pale.

'You don't need to be at the market.'

'But I do.'

'Alina, I am not having you dragging our child….'

It was then he admitted he knew…and Alina simply burst into tears.

'I thought you'd be cross.'

'Cross? Never, ever cross.' He pulled her to him. 'Were you ever going to tell me?'

'Yes,' Alina said, 'when I was over you.'

'He'd be about thirty then!' Demyan said. 'Make that ninety.'

He was so arrogant, so assured as to the depth of her love.

So right.

'We can do better than the market,' he said.

'No!' she wriggled away from him. 'There you go

again, get your cheque book out and buy me a career. You can't imagine how much I'd hate that.'

'I just want to help.'

'I don't need help,' Alina said. 'I don't need you pretending royalty are interested in my painting.'

'What?'

'I know it was you.'

'No!' Demyan's mouth gaped as Alina let out a squeal of horror and then they started to laugh.

'You could be hanging on royal walls.'

'I'll do it my way,' Alina said, but her laughter faded as Demyan continued.

'Did you think long and hard about Dubai?'

'*That* was you?'

'Absolutely! That afternoon, after my mother's service, I got the call from Elizabeth to say that you had turned it down and I knew then you were following your dreams. I told you it was a good day.' He played with her hair. 'Are you nervous about being a stepmother?'

'Demyan…' She lay there. 'You don't have to marry me.'

'Of course I do.'

'Because of the baby?'

'I told you, I don't do that.'

'Yes, but you said that when you already knew that I was pregnant.' That fear was back, fluttering in her chest, leaping in her throat.

'How can you not have faith in us?' Demyan asked.

'I do, but—'

'This is the but,' And at the most inappropriate moment Demyan got out his computer. 'I show you my friends.' He felt the burn of her shame as he pulled up her father's profile and fully exposed her pain.

'Don't…'

'He didn't know you,' Demyan said, 'or he would never have left. I know you and I never could.' He looked at Alina. 'Are we in a relationship?'

'Yes.'

She watched as he clicked the button and then Demyan started to type his first post ever.

Alina and I are pleased to announce...

'Alina, do you want to be my wife?'

She lay there.

'I don't nag.'

'Beg,' she corrected.

'For you I beg,' Demyan said, 'but just this once. Will you please be my wife?'

'What do you think?

'Of course you will,' he said. 'You just have to learn how to say yes.'

'Yes.'

Demyan hadn't known when he'd use it, just that he would.

'Ready to cut those strings?' Demyan checked as he typed.

Alina and I are pleased to announce that we are soon to be married. It will be a small, intimate service, with just the closest of family and friends. We just wanted to share the happy news.

'Ready to soar?' Demyan asked as he handed her the computer.

It was up to Alina to hit Send.

She did.

They were home.

CHAPTER SEVENTEEN

SHE PAINTED HIM with her fingers.

It had been an indecently long honeymoon and now, on their final stop, an island off Far North Queensland, as the sun set on their last day, Alina tried to put the finishing touches to her work, her attempt to capture, on canvas, a chameleon called Demyan.

The sun burnt on her shoulders and their baby slept in her ripe stomach as Demyan lay on the day bed and watched her concentrate and then blush as she painted his dangly bits, which were starting to undangle themselves.

'Stay still,' Alina said. 'I don't usually paint people.'

'I'm bored,' he said, flicking through his tablet.

'You're not.'

'I am and I have a surprise for you…'

'I don't want a surprise.' Alina smiled. 'I *want* to be bored.'

'That I can't do.' He leant over and handed his tablet to her.

Alina stared for a very long moment. There was the princess who had been through their home and she was wearing a dress that Alina would recognise anywhere—not the dress itself but the fabric. The swirls and swirls of poppies she had painted on silk, which was now being worn by royalty.

'Demyan…' She was embarrassed, cross about his meddling but excited too. 'I told you not to interfere, I don't want your help…'

'Alina, I messed them around when I withdrew our home. Of course I had to apologise. I sent some fabric by the artist that the princess had said she liked. Do you think she had it made into a dress to appease me?'

'No.'

'Do you think, if she did not love it, that at best I would have got a polite letter thanking me for her gift?'

'I guess.'

'Clearly, she loves your work. Clearly, because I received a very nice response last night, suggesting I look at the news.'

'And you didn't think to tell me.'

'You wanted to add to your shoe collection,' Demyan said, watching as Alina still stared at the screen, looking at the poppies and remembering the love she had felt as she'd painted.

'When I did this piece I was thinking if it was a girl to call her Poppy.'

'You know what you can do with that thought.'

'It's a lovely name.'

'Poppy Zukov is a stripper's name.'

Alina laughed but then she was serious. 'Can we sort out names or is that bad luck?' There were fewer superstitions these days but plenty of traditions, and they were also making their own, and she wanted their baby named on their honeymoon.

'We can,' Demyan said, 'though we will probably change our minds when it is here.'

'Do you still want a girl?'

'If I had enough energy,' Demyan sighed, 'I would get up from this day bed and smash my head against the

wall. I said that I wanted a girl *once*. When we were discussing Roman I said that maybe if it was a girl it might
be easier, especially if the results were not the news we
wanted. That problem is gone.'

The tests were in. Demyan was Roman's father, in
every way possible. The new baby, if it was a boy, would
be Demyan's second son.

'I said that,' he attempted again to clarify his words,
'just because it might be easier on Roman. I don't care
what we have.' He stroked her stomach. 'I just want him
or her to be here.'

There *was* an advantage to being a second wife that
Alina thought of then—you knew the sort of father that
you were getting for your child.

'So,' Demyan said, 'get it in your head that I have no
preference.'

'None?'

'You found out, didn't you?' Demyan smiled. 'We're
having a boy?'

'No.'

'No, you didn't find out or, no, we're having a girl?'

'Annika.'

The best he had hoped for was that his mother might
rest in peace, but Alina attached a smile to his mother's
name as she returned it to his heart.

'Ya lyublyu tebya vsey dushoy.' Demyan told Alina
just how deeply he loved her and his beautiful mouth
moved into a smile when, instead of the more familiar *I
know you do,* Alina answered him back with a truth he
would never forget.

'As you should.'

* * * * *

REQUEST YOUR FREE BOOKS!

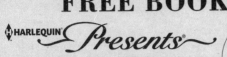

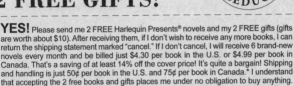

2 FREE NOVELS PLUS
2 FREE GIFTS!

YES! Please send me 2 FREE Harlequin Presents® novels and my 2 FREE gifts (gifts are worth about $10). After receiving them, if I don't wish to receive any more books, I can return the shipping statement marked "cancel." If I don't cancel, I will receive 6 brand-new novels every month and be billed just $4.30 per book in the U.S. or $4.99 per book in Canada. That's a saving of at least 14% off the cover price! It's quite a bargain! Shipping and handling is just 50¢ per book in the U.S. and 75¢ per book in Canada.* I understand that accepting the 2 free books and gifts places me under no obligation to buy anything. I can always return a shipment and cancel at any time. Even if I never buy another book, the two free books and gifts are mine to keep forever.

106/306 HDN FVRK

Name	(PLEASE PRINT)

Address	Apt. #

City	State/Prov.	Zip/Postal Code

Signature (if under 18, a parent or guardian must sign)

Mail to the **Harlequin® Reader Service:**
IN U.S.A.: P.O. Box 1867, Buffalo, NY 14240-1867
IN CANADA: P.O. Box 609, Fort Erie, Ontario L2A 5X3

**Are you a current subscriber to Harlequin Presents books
and want to receive the larger-print edition?
Call 1-800-873-8635 or visit www.ReaderService.com.**

* Terms and prices subject to change without notice. Prices do not include applicable taxes. Sales tax applicable in N.Y. Canadian residents will be charged applicable taxes. Offer not valid in Quebec. This offer is limited to one order per household. Not valid for current subscribers to Harlequin Presents books. All orders subject to credit approval. Credit or debit balances in a customer's account(s) may be offset by any other outstanding balance owed by or to the customer. Please allow 4 to 6 weeks for delivery. Offer available while quantities last.

Your Privacy—The Harlequin® Reader Service is committed to protecting your privacy. Our Privacy Policy is available online at www.ReaderService.com or upon request from the Harlequin Reader Service.

We make a portion of our mailing list available to reputable third parties that offer products we believe may interest you. If you prefer that we not exchange your name with third parties, or if you wish to clarify or modify your communication preferences, please visit us at www.ReaderService.com/consumerschoice or write to us at Harlequin Reader Service Preference Service, P.O. Box 9062, Buffalo, NY 14269. Include your complete name and address.

HPI3

"AND what about us? Where are we supposed to go?" Belle
demanded heatedly, her temper rising. "It takes time to
relocate."

"You'll have at least a month to find somewhere else,"
Cristo fielded without perceptible sympathy while he watched
the breeze push the soft clinging cotton of her top against
her breasts. He clenched his teeth together, willing back his
arousal.

"That's not very long. Five children take up a lot of
space…they're your brothers and sisters, too, so you should
care about what happens to them!" Belle launched back at
him in furious condemnation.

"Which is why I'm here to suggest that we get married and
make a home for them together," Cristo countered with harsh
emphasis as he wondered for possibly the very first time in his
life whether he really did know what he was doing.

"*Married?*" Belle repeated, aghast, wondering if she'd

missed a line or two in the conversation. "What on earth are you talking about?"

"You said that you wanted your siblings to enjoy the Ravelli name and lifestyle. I can only make that happen by marrying you and adopting them."

Frowning in confusion, Belle fell back a step, in too much shock to immediately respond. "Is this a joke?" she asked when she had finally found her voice again.

"It is not," Cristo replied levelly, a stray shard of sunlight breaking through the clouds to slant across his lean, strong face.

All over again, Belle studied him in wonder, because he had the smoldering dark beauty of a fallen angel. His brilliant dark eyes were nothing short of stunning below the thick screen of his lashes, and suddenly she felt breathless.

* * *

The Legacies of Powerful Men

Three tenets to live by: money, power and the ruthless pursuit of passion!

*Available in June 2014,
wherever books and ebooks are sold!*

HARLEQUIN®
Presents®

Revenge and seduction intertwine…

Is gorgeous billionaire Cesar Da Silva finally off the market? Read the final book in Abby Green's gripping Blood Brothers trilogy!

Cesar Da Silva hits the headlines!

Not only are his family secrets about to be exposed, but he's been caught kissing Lexie Anderson!

The reclusive billionaire has certainly smashed his own rules by romancing the high-profile actress, and if their chemistry is anything to go by, this is one match that's bound to be explosive….

WHEN DA SILVA BREAKS THE RULES
by
Abby Green

**Available June 2014,
wherever books and ebooks are sold!**

HP132492